Chestnut Hill

MAKING STRIDES

*Share every moment
with the girls of*

Chestnut Hill

THE NEW CLASS
MAKING STRIDES
HEART OF GOLD

Chestnut Hill

MAKING STRIDES

by **Lauren Brooke**

SCHOLASTIC INC.

New York Toronto London Auckland Sydney
Mexico City New Delhi Hong Kong Buenos Aires

With special thanks to
Elisabeth Faith

ISBN 0-439-73855-5

Chestnut Hill series created by Working Partners Ltd, London.

Copyright © 2005 by Working Partners Ltd.
Published by Scholastic Inc. All rights reserved.

SCHOLASTIC and associated logos are trademarks and/or registered trademarks of Scholastic Inc.

12 11 10 9 8 7 6 5 4 3 2 1   5 6 7 8 9 10/0
Printed in the U.S.A.   40
First printing, November 2005

CHAPTER ONE

Malory O'Neil groaned as a buzzer sounded in the hallway outside her room. "You've got to be kidding," she said, checking the clock on her bedside table. It was one minute after eight. *"Come on! It's Saturday."*

"Someone should complain to Mrs. Herson," agreed Lani Hernandez, who shared the dorm room with Malory and Alexandra Cooper.

"You do it. You're closer to the door," Malory pointed out before snuggling farther under her covers. She shouted with laughter as a pillow landed squarely on her face. She loved the weekends at Chestnut Hill — and not just because normally she could sleep in. Without regular classes, she could spend as much time in the stables as she wanted. Or she could just hang out with her friends. *Maybe if it's nice we could get permission to go on a trail ride*, Malory thought. Suddenly her eyes flew open. *Oh, no! How could I have forgotten what today is?*

There was a quick knock, and the door opened. Mrs. Herson, the housemother for the underclassmen of Adams House, stepped into the room. "Didn't you hear the first buzzer half an hour ago?"

"I guess we must have slept through that one." Lani tried to explain. Their other dorm mate, Alexandra Cooper, was already dressed and sitting at the desk next to her bed with headphones on. Her shoulder-length hair swung around her face as she leaned over her textbook, totally engrossed.

"I need you at breakfast in five minutes sharp," Mrs. Herson told them. She strode across the room to Alexandra and placed a hand on her shoulder. Alex looked up and quickly pulled the headphones from her ears. "Have you forgotten it's Homecoming Weekend, and you all have responsibilities? Please hurry." Without waiting for their reply, she left the room.

Lani and Malory raised their eyebrows at each other. "Whoa. Now we know how Mrs. Herson operates under stress," Lani said, voicing Malory's exact thoughts.

Under most circumstances, their housemother was always composed and fair. *She didn't give me a detention for tracking mud into the entrance hall yesterday*, Malory remembered, feeling grateful that it had been the calm, collected Mrs. Herson whom she had dealt with then. Not wanting to push her luck, Malory hurried out of bed and rummaged for something to wear. She pulled out some

Levi's and a green T-shirt, tugging them on before tying her dark brown hair back. She couldn't resist sneaking a peek out of the window while she coaxed her unbrushed waves into a tidy knot. The view looked straight over the turnout paddocks on the edge of the campus. There were only a few faculty horses grazing in the early fall sunshine. The others were in the barn, waiting to be groomed for the exhibition ride later.

Malory felt a nervous tingle shoot up her spine. She had earned her place on the junior jumping team only the week before. Since then the five team members had been practicing nonstop for the Homecoming exhibition. She leaned her forehead against the glass for a moment. She couldn't believe that she'd nearly missed the tryouts altogether. She'd been in the middle of packing her bags to leave Chestnut Hill, convinced she would never fit in, when her classmate Dylan Walsh had found her and persuaded her to give the boarding school — and the other students — one more chance.

Malory smiled as she remembered how Dylan, who was the reserve member of the team, had flown around her last practice course on Morello. The pair had looked exceptional and Malory had no doubt that they'd be impressive today. But the Alumnae demonstration wasn't just for fun — it was a chance to see how the team members performed under pressure. In just three weeks they would have their first interschool competition.

Always slow to rise, Lani finally kicked her covers off and stretched her arms over her head. "Hey, Alex. Why didn't you wake us?" Lani asked as she grabbed a pair of pants from the pile of clothes at the bottom of her bed.

"Sorry." Alexandra closed her book and added it to a stack on the corner of her desk. "I didn't hear the bell, either. I had my headphones on to drown out your snoring."

Lani looked at Alex in surprise. "Isn't it a little early in the morning for sarcasm?"

Alexandra shrugged. "I've been up for a while."

Malory laughed to herself, realizing her two room-mates didn't really understand each other. Alexandra was the serious student, while Lani was in for serious fun. Malory gave Lani an understanding smile and then glanced at the open notebook on Alex's desk. "What are you working on?"

"The English assignment on female poets Ms. Griffiths gave us yesterday. I thought I'd get started on Sylvia Plath. She's just so amazing, I guess I lost track of time."

"Well, even poets have to eat!" Malory reminded her. "Let's go before everyone beats us to the pancakes."

"Yeah," said Lani. "I'm starving!"

🐾

Malory pushed open the swinging doors and breathed in the smell of fresh bread. The cafeteria in the student center had floor-to-ceiling windows looking out over the grounds and picnic area, which looked tranquil with a light cover of autumn dew. But the dining hall was another story, buzzing with noise and activity.

Dylan waved at Malory and the others from across the cafeteria. She was sitting at a table opposite her roommate, Honey Harper. Despite their initial issues, Malory now felt closer to Dylan than any of the other girls. It had meant a lot to her that Dylan had wanted her to stay at Chestnut Hill. Malory liked Honey a lot, too. Sometimes Honey's English accent made her sound reserved and a little aloof, but Malory knew better. With her roommates close behind, Malory weaved her way through the tables and chairs.

"Hey, guys, you'd better grab some breakfast before they close the kitchen," Dylan warned. Her green eyes sparkled mischievously. "But I hate to tell you, gruel is the only thing on the menu."

Malory looked at Dylan's tray, stunned. The catering staff always served great breakfasts on the weekends: any style of eggs, French toast, waffles, muffins, three kinds of sausage, and lots of fresh fruit. Dylan always took some of everything, but today she had a lone bowl with a pasty substance on the bottom.

"Well, technically they're calling it maple oatmeal." Honey smiled.

"You've got to be kidding," Alexandra groaned.

"Nope. The dining hall staff is working overtime on the Homecoming buffet. And we're not even invited — alumnae only. It's a good thing it happens only once a year or they might find themselves with a riot on their hands," Dylan told them, running her finger around the top of her café latte and licking it. *At least the coffee machine is still available*, Malory thought.

"I'll start a formal petition!" Lani grabbed Alex's notebook and pretended to take down names.

"Come on, guys." Malory laughed. "Let's go check out this gruel."

By the time they had filled their bowls with oatmeal and returned to their table, the hall was starting to empty. Girls had scattered in multiple directions to prepare for the day's events. In addition to the riding exhibition, there would be performances by the drama and choral groups and the orchestra. There was also an art show in the campus gallery, as well as tours by the students and faculty.

"I hope we get the same five-star treatment when we come back after graduation," Lani pretended to grumble.

"Speaking of five-star treatment," Dylan added, "Miss Lynsey Harrison is headed our way. Do you think we should make room?"

"That's okay. I've finished," Honey replied, standing up.

She picked up her half-full bowl and carried it to

the dirty-dish rack, passing Lynsey, Patience Duvall, and Razina Jackson, who were coming the opposite way. Lynsey looked predictably immaculate in a pale blue cashmere sweater, embroidered skirt, and matching blue suede boots. Patience, as usual, was just two steps behind Lynsey, while Razina casually swung by the coffee station before joining the others.

Malory felt herself flinch as Lynsey approached. She couldn't help but feel intimidated by Lynsey, and Malory was sure the other girl was well aware of that fact.

"So," Lynsey said to Dylan and Malory. "Are you ready for the exhibition? Do you have your shirts pressed and boots polished?"

Malory shifted in her chair. Lynsey's riding uniform was as classy as the rest of her wardrobe. Rumor had it that she had all her clothes made for her by an equestrian outfitter on New York's Upper East Side. Malory's store-bought jacket and breeches couldn't begin to compare. Fortunately not all the girls on the junior team were as focused on that aspect of their presentation as Lynsey; they were much more concerned about the riding itself. No one wanted the alumnae to go home thinking Chestnut Hill's standards were anything but the best, especially not when they had a new Director of Riding, Ali Carmichael.

"Are your sisters coming to watch you ride?" Alexandra asked Lynsey when Malory and Dylan didn't answer.

"Yes, Rachel was captain of the senior riding team last year," Lynsey replied. "My other sister, Sienna, will be here today, too. They are both very competitive, so I really want us to be on."

Malory and Dylan rolled their eyes. With her nearly perfect pony, Bluegrass, Lynsey was one of the most promising riders for Chestnut Hill. Plus, all the women in her family had graduated from the elite school, and her father had attended the prestigious boys' school Saint Christophers, which was just on the other side of town. Malory and Dylan didn't need to be reminded that their teammate had a blue-blooded legacy.

"Have you checked your riding stuff?" Lynsey pestered. She raised her thinly plucked blonde eyebrows in Dylan and Malory's direction.

"Our hairnets are all ready to go," said Dylan, her expression deadly serious. After all, wearing a hairnet under your helmet was a necessary, yet far from glamorous, demand of showing. "And we spent most of last night shining our boots. I'm just about all out of spit now."

"Dylan Walsh, you are so gross." Lynsey rolled her eyes as the others burst into laughter.

"Are you nervous, Dylan?" Razina leaned forward, flicking her long, black braids back over her shoulders.

"I dreamed last night that I was the only member of the team to knock down a jump," Dylan admitted. "I went clear until the last fence, and then Morello refused and sent me flying over the top of it. And since I'm the reserve rider, I'm only taking part in the jumping round. Think how freaked I'd be if I was riding in the dressage demonstration like everyone else!"

Malory smiled. She knew that secretly Dylan would have loved to be doing the dressage quadrille, even though it would have meant a double dose of nerves. The quadrille required that the four horses and riders move through their gaits in time with choreography and music. It unnerved Malory to have to be so in sync with the others, but, like Dylan, her bad dreams had been about the jumping course. "My subconscious was working overtime, too," Malory confessed. "I dreamed we kept getting slower and slower until Hardy was walking through all of the fences!"

"Like that's going to happen," Dylan said loyally.

Malory flashed her friend a grin. It was nice to have Dylan's support.

"You do know we're wearing the tan breeches this afternoon, right?" Lynsey questioned.

Malory wondered if Lynsey was going to ask about every last piece of clothing and tack.

"Lynsey, we have a checklist of everything we need to do to get ready for the demonstration," said Dylan, her voice edged with exasperation. "But nowhere did it say we had to answer your questions. It's fine if you're nervous, but don't take it out on us."

"I'm not nervous!" Lynsey snapped. "I only wanted to

make sure that you guys were prepared, since you are both new to riding at this level. I won't bother next time."

"Oh, no!" Dylan retorted. "How will we ever manage without you?"

Malory noticed Dylan's green eyes darken to hazel, a sure sign that she was about to lose her temper. But Lynsey waved off Dylan's comment, and both girls made a point of looking away. Malory was amazed that the two managed to live in the same dorm room. It seemed tense enough when they were in public. They often bickered with each other, yet Malory thought they had an understanding, too. They seemed to get away with insults that neither would tolerate from anyone else.

Things had been bad between them almost from the beginning, but they got worse when Lynsey had trash-talked Malory because her dad owned a small-town shoe store. Dylan said she couldn't forgive Lynsey for that.

Malory was pulled from her thoughts when Mrs. Herson appeared at the table. "You had better get a move on, girls," she said sternly. "We've only got an hour before the alums start arriving."

The girls hurriedly gulped the last of their coffee and juice, then pushed back their chairs.

Malory thought of Hardy waiting in his stall alongside Dylan's favorite pony, Morello. She grinned at her friend. "Come on. We've got dates with two cute boys. They're waiting for us in the barn."

"I just hope my date didn't sleep in manure again last night," Dylan replied with a groan.

"No worries," Malory assured Dylan, sounding more confident than she felt. "We have plenty of time and fresh hairnets to spare. What could go wrong?"

CHAPTER TWO

Malory felt her spirits lift as she headed down the path toward the stable block. She had split up with Dylan and Lani after Honey had convinced all three of them to help post the Homecoming itinerary flyers around the academic buildings. Malory was amazed what Honey could con them into with her polished British accent. Now that Malory had taped up her stack of flyers, she was on her way to see Hardy. She took a deep breath of the brisk autumn air and looked around. She loved the setup at Chestnut Hill, with a traditional stone-built stable block opposite the big wooden barn, flanked by indoor and outdoor arenas.

I wish Mom could have seen all this, Malory thought. Her mom had died two years ago, and she still couldn't kick the habit of longing to share moments with her. *Maybe I never will.* Her lips tugged up in a smile as she thought back to her first day of elementary school. Her mom had made her a special breakfast of blueberry pancakes with whipped cream to mark the special occasion; but the batch took too long to cook and mother and daughter had too much fun slurping up the whipped cream. Of course, Malory had been late and missed her bus, and her mom, in her robe and pajamas, had to drive her to school. But Mrs. O'Neil didn't flinch when the principal, Mrs. Zenisak, strode out to the sedan to say hello. *I'd have loved seeing Lynsey's face if Mom had done the same thing on the first day at Chestnut Hill.*

Malory's smile turned into a grin, and she hurried into the barn.

"Hi, Malory!" called Kelly, one of the full-time stable hands, as she sped past with an armful of tack. "I saw Dylan and Lani head in a few minutes ago." Kelly just managed to avoid colliding with the other stable hand, Sarah, who was pushing a wheelbarrow in the opposite direction.

When Malory looked down the stable aisle, it was like a circus, but sure enough, she saw Dylan, Lani, and Honey toward the far end of the barn, just as Kelly had promised. Malory headed for the group, passing girls with everything from brushes to boot polish and braiding yarn in their hands.

Bluegrass, Lynsey's beautiful blue roan, pricked his ears and gave a low call as she sped down the center aisle. Malory usually slipped him a treat when she came to see Hardy. "Sorry, boy, I can't stop," she called. "I'm sure Lynsey will be down to see to you soon."

"Has anyone seen Snap's saddle?" Clare Houlder, an upperclassman who was giving a jumping demonstration on Snapdragon, stuck her head out of the tack room.

Dylan shook her head. "If it's not in there, I don't know where it would be."

"Camilla's already tacking Snapdragon up. She's giving a dressage demonstration on him before Clare," said Kelly.

"What?" Clare appeared looking totally hassled, with her hands on her hips.

"She's riding before you are," Lani explained. "Didn't you check the schedule?"

"Schedule, schmedule," Clare retorted, totally unaware that Ali Carmichael had just walked into the barn.

Yikes! Malory thought.

"I'll have you know that blood, sweat, and tears have gone into the arrangements for today," Ms. Carmichael announced.

Clare spun around, her cheeks turning scarlet.

"And if you'd like to check the *schmedule*," Ms. Carmichael went on, tapping her pen against her clipboard, "you'll see that for those of you who are sharing ponies, the rider going first is tacking up, and the second rider will make any tack adjustments before her turn. If the second riders want to help with the grooming, that's fine; but Kelly and Sarah will be primarily responsible for this. I know you all have duties up at the school this morning."

"Yes, Ms. Carmichael," Clare said meekly.

Malory looked at Dylan, curious if her friend was surprised by their trainer's tone. Dylan didn't say much about her aunt being their riding instructor, but Malory was sure it was tricky sometimes.

When Malory stepped into Hardy's stall, he blinked at her sleepily from where he was lying in his bed of sweet-smelling straw.

"Come on, lazy!" She laughed as Hardy heaved himself to his feet and shook off the strands of straw. Malory unbuckled his stable rug and was relieved to find him clean underneath it. All he needed was a quick once-over with the body brush and polishing with a stable rubber to be ready for the ring.

She was just running her fingers through Hardy's tail to ease out any tangles when she heard a groan from the stall next door. "What's up?" she asked, standing on tiptoe to look over the partition.

Morello's stable rug was folded over his door, and Dylan and Lani were peering in dismay at his brown-and-white flank.

"We've tried everything to get this mark out, but it's only getting worse," Dylan complained, pointing to a greenish stain on a patch of white hair.

"It's the incredible, growing manure stain," Lani declared, but Dylan didn't even crack a smile.

"We haven't even combed his mane for braiding!" Dylan's voice rose in panic.

"Calm down, or you'll freak Morello out," Malory warned as she noticed the paint gelding shift restlessly.

Dylan took several deep breaths and ran her hand down Morello's neck. "Sorry, boy," she told him. "I'm just having a nervous breakdown, that's all. Nothing for you to worry about, I promise."

Malory ducked down so Dylan wouldn't see her broad grin. She didn't want her friend to think she was unsympathetic, but it was hard not to laugh when she was being deliberately melodramatic!

Ms. Carmichael came up the aisle and stopped outside Morello's stall. "There'll be no nervous breakdowns on my yard. You can go back to your room and have one there."

"But look at him. He's nowhere near ready!" Dylan protested, gesturing to the pony's stained side. "I need a professional car wash to get this mark off, or maybe a Laundromat. I don't know which is better."

"Dylan, relax," Ms. Carmichael advised. She took a deep breath and looked at her niece. "My staff is more than capable of getting the horses ready for this afternoon. Or we would be if we were left to our work and not harassed by stressed-out students." Ms. Carmichael crossed her arms. "All you girls have been asked to do is make sure the ponies are tacked up in time."

"But —"

"No buts. Just leave. I don't want the boarding-house staff down here looking for you. They have more than enough to do today. Don't come back until one o'clock."

❧

Don't worry, Dylan. Your aunt's totally in control," Lani commented as the three girls obediently left the barn. "I bet she has the ponies looking like they're ready for the Olympics by the time you get back."

Malory had just enough time to give Hardy a light brush and put his stable sheet back on before Ms. Carmichael had banished them from the stable.

Dylan sighed. "You're right. I'm just letting every-thing get to me. Morello still struggles with the first fence of every combination. And he hates that fence just off the corner. I mean, what will I say to Ali if I'm the only one who doesn't jump a clear round?"

"At least you get your canter transitions right," Malory pointed out. "I haven't been able to get Hardy to strike off on the correct lead for the last three quadrille practices. I can just hear people saying, 'Why did they ever give her the scholarship?'" Malory had earned her place at Chestnut Hill after being spotted by Diane

Rockwell, one of the school's graduates who went on to compete on the national team. Ms. Rockwell had asked Malory to try out for her grant — a six-year scholarship to Chestnut Hill. Malory could still hardly believe she'd been given such an incredible opportunity to improve her skills in one of the best riding programs in the country, but some days — like today — she wasn't convinced she deserved it at all.

"Enough already!" Lani agreed. "You're starting to make me feel nervous, and I'm not even riding!"

"Okay, I promise not to say anything else about which leg Hardy starts cantering on again," Malory said solemnly. "But I can't promise that I won't worry about him jumping flat," she continued, bursting into laughter as Lani grabbed her shoulders and gave her a strong, yet affectionate, shake.

Malory threw back her head and took in a deep breath of air that was sweet with the scent of newly cut grass. *How bad could it be, riding in front of the Chestnut Hill alumnae? They certainly knew all about feeling under pressure. They can't all be as perfect and as confident as Lynsey Harrison, can they . . . ?*

🐎

By eleven-thirty it seemed every room in every building in the school was overrun with visitors.

"I think I must have served five hundred cups of mint

tea," Malory gasped. She looked down at the buffet table, which was still covered with silver trays holding the remains of olives, stuffed mushrooms, swiss cheese croquettes, and shrimp hors d'oeuvres. Dylan offered her the tray of tiny cucumber sandwiches she had been serving around the hall.

"I couldn't eat a thing," Malory confessed. "My stomach's full of butterflies just now." She could do with a sip of one of the herbal teas her mom had brewed whenever she was nervous. Malory had never been able to figure out whether it was the bramble tea or the way her mom could always make the scariest situation funny in some way that had eased her nerves.

"Have you seen Lynsey's sisters anywhere?" Dylan asked, helping Malory to stack the teacups. "I was half expecting them to be parading around with flashing neon signs."

Malory grinned. "Careful. If Lynsey hears you, she'll flip. You know darn well that no Harrison would be caught within fifty feet of a neon sign."

"You've got me there. Where is she, anyhow? Did she manage to get out of wait-staff duty because she has guests?"

"I haven't seen her since breakfast," Malory confessed. "Which suits me fine. I don't need any reminders of all the ways I could botch things up this afternoon."

"You can always count on Lynsey," Dylan agreed.

Making sure the coast was clear, she popped an hors d'oeuvre into her mouth, then made a hideous face. "Ugh, anchovy!"

"Here." Malory shoved a napkin into Dylan's hand and turned to block her from Mrs. Herson's eagle eye as she spit out the unsavory hors d'oeuvre.

"Let's just hope lunch is better," Dylan croaked, folding the napkin and dropping it into a trash can. "I'm starving!"

Wei Lin, who shared a dorm room with Patience and Razina, stopped on her way to the kitchen, carrying a tray loaded with half-empty jugs of juice and mineral water. "Have you heard? We're confined to our dorm for lunch. The upperclassmen called dibs on the picnic tables, the alumnae are eating in the dining hall, and so we are relegated to our dining room."

"No way," Dylan said indignantly.

Wei Lin nodded, tucking her shining black hair behind her ears. "I'm afraid so. But don't worry. Just a couple more years, and we'll be forcing someone else to eat off their laps!"

Two alumnae walked up with empty cups, each with a different shade of lipstick smudged against the rim. One of the women smiled at Malory as she handed over her cup before turning to the blond beside her. "Naomi and I are going to watch the tennis match, are you coming?"

"Actually, Martina and I are interested in the drama

presentation," replied the blond. "I can't believe Ms. Sinclair is still here. Talk about school loyalty. I bet she's every bit as inspiring as she used to be."

"What do you think — lawyers?" Malory whispered as the women stalked away on their Prada heels.

"Bankers," Wei Lin decided. "They look just like the type of people my mom works with." Wei Lin's mom was the financial director of a major insurance company.

Dylan shook her head. "Too obvious. I figure they're private eyes with a monster clothing budget so they can mix with high society."

Malory smirked as she glanced at her watch. "We'd better go and change into our riding gear," she warned Dylan. There was a chance she'd feel better once she was wearing her breeches and black jacket, but she somehow doubted it. It wasn't only her own reputation that was at stake. Malory knew that Dylan's aunt had been a controversial choice to replace the former Director of Riding, Elizabeth Mitchell. Ms. Mitchell had been adored — in part because her riders claimed countless blue ribbons and gold trophies for Chestnut Hill. Coming from a newer stable in Lexington, Kentucky, Ms. Carmichael didn't have a polished track record on the East Coast competition circuit. There would be a legion of returning team riders watching the demonstrations, including Lynsey's sister Rachel, all curious to see if the new riding director could cut it. As the newest riding recruits, it was up to Malory and the rest of the junior team to prove that she could!

🙤

Mrs. Herson set down a large box on the sitting-room table. "Sorry, girls, but you'll have to help yourselves to lunch," she announced. "I need to get back to the cafeteria. It's like a war zone over there!"

"The alumnae are getting silver service, no doubt," Lani murmured.

Two of the catering staff set down a basket of fruit and a cooler of bottled water and juice before following Mrs. Herson out.

Malory waited for the rush of girls to ease before she went up to the table. "Is that all you're having?" Dylan asked when Malory joined her in the drinks line.

Malory glanced down at her lonely cheese sandwich. "I guess I'm too nervous to eat," she admitted.

Dylan's plate was loaded with several sandwiches, chips, and fruit. "That's too bad. Whenever I get nervous I eat like a horse!"

"Speaking of which, it's quarter to one. Ms. Carmichael told us to be down on the yard in fifteen minutes," Malory pointed out.

"Yikes!" Dylan picked up a sandwich and bit into it, then headed to the corner of the room where Alex, Wei

Lin, Lani, Honey, and Razina were sitting cross-legged, balancing their plates on their laps.

"I'm so glad I didn't have to do anything for the drama department," Razina said. "That's the good thing about being in our first year." Then seeing Dylan and Malory, she gave them a sheepish smile. "What time are you riding?"

"In an hour," Dylan answered.

"A bunch of us are planning on coming down to cheer you on," Alex said.

"Thanks." Malory hoped she wasn't about to mess up in front of her entire dorm in addition to the alumnae. "I can't eat this," Malory said, looking down at her sandwich. "I'm going to head down to the yard."

"Honey and I will come give you a hand." Lani jumped up and brushed the crumbs off her lap.

Dylan stuffed her pockets with two apples.

"Good luck," their friends called as they left the room. "We'll be rooting for you all the way!"

Malory and Honey left Lani and Dylan with Morello and went to check on Hardy. The chestnut gelding was tied up at the back of the stall so he wouldn't get himself dirty, but he swung his head around and nickered at the sound of Malory's voice. "Hello, boy. Don't you look gorgeous!" She scratched Hardy gently behind his ears. Hearing the clatter of a grooming kit being dropped, Malory placed her hand flat on Hardy's nose to calm him.

"Sorry!" Paige Rivers called from her pony Rose's stall.

Malory kept her hand on Hardy until she felt him relax. "I think I might go see if they ever got Morello's stain out before I start tacking up," she told Honey.

Honey smiled. "Ah, the stain of doom."

"That would be the one." Malory laughed. She slipped out of the stall with Honey right behind.

"I'll grab your tack," Honey offered.

"Thanks." Malory took a deep breath, trying not to feel frazzled by everyone else's nerves.

When she reached Morello's stall, Malory saw Aiden Phillips, the jumping coach, crouched down next to the pony's flank. Straightening up, Aiden made a grand gesture toward her handiwork. "Ta-dah," she said, grasping a piece of dressmaker's chalk in her hand. The white patch looked bright enough to be on a laundry detergent commercial.

"That's fantastic!" Dylan enthused. "Who knew chalk would come to our rescue?"

"If you have a paint pony, you should keep some in your tack trunk," Aiden suggested.

"You know, if Lynsey saw how well that worked, she'd probably tell you to use the chalk all over," Malory said.

She knew Dylan loved the contrast of Morello's chestnut and snow-white coat, but Lynsey seemed to think paints were second-class show ponies.

"Okay then," said Aiden, choosing to ignore Malory's jab at Lynsey. "Can I trust you to take care of tack? There's so much doubling up today, I just hope everyone shows up on the right horse at the right time." She grabbed her clipboard, which she'd left on the half-wall.

"You need more ponies," Dylan joked.

"You're not wrong," the trainer agreed. "The riding program's more popular than ever this year, and Ms. Carmichael said she's seriously thinking about buying some new horses."

Malory caught Dylan's eye and raised her eyebrows. What could be better than more horses at Chestnut Hill?

"Has anyone seen Lynsey?" Ms. Carmichael stopped in front of Morello's stall and looked expectantly at the jumping coach and junior-team riders.

"Um, she's on her way," Malory said. She winked at Dylan as Ms. Carmichael and Ms. Phillips headed off together. "She's probably getting her sisters prime seats in the arena," Malory added.

"Serves her right if she's not ready in time," Dylan replied as she scooped a brush out of the bucket and began to draw it over Morello's coat.

"Thanks a lot, Dylan. That's a great team attitude."

Lynsey was standing in the doorway. She looked immaculate with her long leather boots gleaming against her pale tan breeches. She glanced down and flicked a piece of hay off her tailored black coat.

Malory noticed that she looked pale under her hard hat, and Lynsey's fingers had definitely trembled as she dropped the hay into the drainage gully. "If you're running late, I can help you tack up Bluegrass," she offered. "Honey can take care of Hardy."

"I've already got Patience helping me out. If you've got time on your hands, why don't you go practice cantering on the right leg?" Lynsey suggested sweetly.

Malory counted to ten under her breath as her classmate headed out of the stall. *If I get stressed, it will be bad for Hardy. He'll only pick up on it and get nervous.*

"Here you go." Honey appeared with her arms full of Morello's tack. "I've put Hardy's over his door," she added.

"Thanks, Honey," said Dylan, stuffing the brush back into the bucket. "And Mal, ignore our dear friend Lynsey Harrison. Just concentrate on making Hardy look great, and she'll only be sorry when you outshine her in the demonstration!"

Malory smiled and wished she could be as confident about her performance as her friend.

When she finally led Hardy onto the yard, she had to admit he looked magnificent. He wasn't finely bred like

Bluegrass or strikingly colored like Morello, but the chestnut cob arched his neck proudly and pricked his ears like a nineteenth-century portrait of a hunter. The rest of the junior-team members were already mounted and waiting for her by the entrance.

"Do you want me to hold him while you get on?" Dylan asked. She had left Morello in his stall because she wasn't riding until the jumping part of the demonstration later on.

"Thanks." Malory let Dylan hold Hardy's reins while she swung herself into the saddle. As soon as she settled her feet into the stirrups and sat up straight, she felt her heart flip over with pride — plus a healthy dose of disbelief. She couldn't believe she was about to represent Chestnut Hill! When she'd e-mailed her dad about it the day before, he'd told her how proud he was of her; and how proud her mom would have been, too. She glanced down at the Chestnut Hill crest on her borrowed jacket and touched it lightly with her gloved hand, like it was a lucky charm. She couldn't wait to get her own team jacket.

"We're going to find our seats now," Honey said, smiling up at her.

"Good luck," Lani added.

Dylan stood back to admire the full effect. "You look amazing!"

"Thanks," said Malory, meaning it.

"I was talking to Hardy," Dylan joked before rushing off with the others.

Malory rode Hardy over to the entrance of the arena where Ms. Carmichael was about to address the whole junior team. Bluegrass was looking uncharacteristically anxious. He snatched at his bit and swished his tail.

"Stand still!" Lynsey snapped when the blue roan side-stepped.

"It's perfectly normal for the ponies to be picking up on your nerves," Ms. Carmichael said calmly. "But we've practiced this routine so many times, you'll know exactly where you're going once you're in the arena, and your horses will follow your focus."

Olivia Buckley, an eighth-grader from Walker House who was riding the blue-gray Connemara mare Shamrock, gave a weak smile. "Remind me again, which way do Eleanor and I turn when we ride in through the doors?"

"Right — and you'll be fine. It's just the same as in the schooling ring," Ms. Carmichael assured her. "You all look fantastic. So do the ponies. Just think of this as a practice with added polish, okay?"

The opening chords of their music blared on the other side of the big double doors, and Malory felt her stomach flip over.

Eleanor Dixon shortened Skylark's reins and grinned

around at everyone. "Let's go!" She nudged Skylark forward until she was standing right by the doors. Olivia brought Shamrock alongside her.

Malory squeezed Hardy to stand beside Bluegrass. She glanced sideways at Lynsey and gave her what she hoped was an encouraging smile. *She looks as pale as I feel,* she thought.

She dropped her hand down onto Hardy's shoulder, massaging her fingers in the circular movement she'd been practicing to relax him. Suddenly she couldn't wait to ride into the arena. This was it! She was about to become part of Chestnut Hill's respected riding tradition.

CHAPTER THREE

❧

Ready?" Eleanor glanced over her shoulder at Malory and Lynsey. Skylark pulled at her bit, grazing her teeth against the metal. She had been a top show-jumping pony in her prime, and always picked up on the electric atmosphere of the ring.

"Ready," Malory replied, shortening Hardy's reins. He felt tense and didn't flick his ear as usual at the sound of her voice. "Steady, boy," she soothed as Skylark and Shamrock disappeared into the indoor arena and turned onto the right rein.

"Come on," Lynsey snapped. "You know we've got to keep close together."

Malory listened to the chords in the music for their cue, keeping an eye on Bluegrass as they trotted forward so that Hardy's pace matched exactly. They passed under the massive doorway and turned to the left. Malory gulped. The viewing gallery above the arena was packed fuller than she had ever seen, had ever imagined. She scanned the rows, looking for the supportive smiles of any of the Adams House girls, and then gave up. There were just too many faces.

She shifted her weight in the saddle as they approached the corner of the arena, warning Hardy that she wanted him to turn down the diagonal. The pony felt stiff against her legs. "Nice and easy," she muttered, keeping Lynsey and Bluegrass in the corner of her eye. She closed her legs on Hardy's flanks to lengthen his stride, which was a little shorter than Blue's.

Malory watched the other ponies as they turned to trot across the arena. Just as the drums began to beat, she and Lynsey were supposed to be passing to the right of Eleanor and Olivia. She heard the audience gasp as the riders looked as if they were about to collide. When they passed they were so close that Malory heard the clink of the iron as her stirrup brushed against Eleanor's. As the crowd burst into applause, Malory caught Eleanor's eye, and they swapped broad grins. Hardy snorted as if he was beginning to enjoy himself, too.

When they turned into the corner for the canter strike-off, Malory's heart flipped. This was the part she'd kept messing up in each practice. She sat deep and gave Hardy the firmest signal she could with her outside leg. As if he wouldn't dream of using anything but the correct leg, Hardy struck off perfectly. On the other side of the arena, Shamrock and Skylark cantered in a mirror image of Hardy and Bluegrass. The whole audience was hushed, so the only noise was the rhythmic thudding of the ponies' hooves on the sand.

At the top Malory turned Hardy into the center, hearing Bluegrass snatch at his bit as Lynsey slowed him to keep him exactly alongside. The girls pinwheeled the four horses shoulder to shoulder as the music reached a crescendo. Then moving in complete unison, they halted in a line and reined back. "One, two, three, four," Malory counted under her breath. "We're done!" She dropped Hardy's reins for their bow, and then spoiled the very controlled image of sophistication by bending down to give him a big pat on the neck.

The bleachers erupted in applause, and Malory grinned up at the audience. She smiled even broader when she caught sight of Dylan leaning over the balcony in the far corner. The rest of the Adams students were seated close to her.

The music struck up again, quieter this time, and Malory and Lynsey trotted down the center line in the opposite direction from Eleanor and Olivia. All four ponies circled the arena and met at the main doors with perfect timing. The horses' hooves clattered as they hit the yard, adding to the sound of cheers that followed them out. Malory only had time to drop her stirrups and slip off Hardy when Dylan raced over.

"You guys looked great!" she said breathlessly.

"What did you do, fly down?" Malory laughed. She pulled Hardy's reins over his head and led him out of the way of the intermediate team that was preparing to enter the ring. "You were amazing," she told the chestnut pony, rubbing his nose. She chuckled as Hardy rubbed his head against her arm, wanting his bridle taken off. "Wait until you're in your stall!"

They led Hardy into the barn, and Malory rubbed him down while Dylan went to fill a small hay net, just to keep him quiet. Malory took Hardy's water bucket out of the stall since he was jumping later. *There's no way I'm taking a chance on him getting colic*, she thought. She dunked a sponge into the water and rinsed Hardy's mouth so he wouldn't get thirsty.

Dylan finished tying the hay net to a ring on the wall. "If we get back to the arena at warp speed, we should be in time for the intermediate dressage display."

"I'm right with you," Malory said, patting Hardy's neck before hurrying out of the stall.

"Lani saved seats for us," Dylan puffed as they went around to the side entrance. Malory stepped back to let Dylan go first and then climbed the wooden staircase that led to the bleachers. The girls squeezed down to the bench where Lani was waiting.

"Well done, Mal," Razina said. She was sitting with Wei Lin and Honey on the other side of Lani. She held out a huge bucket of popcorn.

"No thanks." Malory shook her head, knowing her stomach wouldn't settle until she had finished her jumping round as well.

Everyone around them began to clap, and Malory looked down onto the arena to see the senior riding team captain, Sara Chappell, ride in on her own horse, Mischief Maker. Malory was used to seeing Sara ride the bay gelding in short stirrups and jumping gear since he was a talented show-jumper. He looked totally different in a double bridle with no martingale, and a straight-cut dressage saddle.

"Wow!" breathed Dylan. Sara looked so formal in her tailcoat, top hat, and long riding boots. She halted and saluted before sending Mischief Maker into a trot down the center of the arena.

Sara rode the Medium level test perfectly. When Mischief half pirouetted before sliding effortlessly into a collected trot, Malory had to stop herself from giving a cheer. She was excited to overhear words of praise from the alumnae seated in the rows behind her.

"Did we look that good when we rode here?"

"The new Director of Riding obviously has a great dressage program."

"I wouldn't be surprised to see that pair on an international team before too long."

As Sara walked out of the arena on a loose rein, the grounds maintenance team ran in and began setting out a course of eight jumps.

"Check out how high they're building that wall," Dylan whispered. "The combination is as tall as Morello. I hope they lower them for us."

Malory nodded and took a deep breath.

"We'd better run," Dylan hissed, tugging at Malory's sleeve.

Malory wanted to stay and watch the senior team go over the fences, but she knew that Dylan was right — if they didn't hurry, they wouldn't be ready in time for their own jumping demonstration.

"Break a leg," Lani whispered as Malory passed her. "Between you and Hardy, you'll have enough to choose from!"

🐎

Malory and Dylan quickly put Morello and Hardy's bridles on and tightened their girths before leading them out of the barn to the schooling ring.

Olivia and Eleanor walked Shamrock and Skylark around the yard. The intermediate riders were still in the arena. They were doing pretty well if the applause drifting out through the doors was anything to go by.

Hardy tried to turn back to the barn. "Whoa," Malory called, reining him in. "Just one course, and you can have the rest of the day off," she promised.

Malory and Dylan both put their ponies through the paces on the flat and then went over the practice fence a couple of times. Satisfied that Hardy was warmed up, Malory walked him toward the gate. She smiled when Dylan joined her, thinking she had never seen her friend look so serious.

As they headed toward the arena, there was a burst of cheering, and the intermediate team members clattered out. "That will be for you in a couple of minutes," Malory told Hardy with a pat.

"Good luck," wished Anita Demarco, trotting past on her chestnut gelding, Prince. "Watch out for the combination. It's very tight."

"Yikes," Dylan gulped. "That's already my worst fence!"

"You'll be fine," Malory told her friend. "Morello's stride is shorter than Prince's anyway. Just remember to half-halt before you take the corner. You hit it perfectly in the tryouts. There's no reason why you can't do it again."

"Unless it was a fluke," Lynsey said as she walked Bluegrass toward the entrance.

Malory looked up, shocked. Lynsey always seemed to appear out of nowhere to catch them with their defenses down.

Before either girl could respond, the loudspeaker blared, "And now for our last demonstration of the afternoon, given by the junior jumping team."

"Let's go show them what we've got," grinned Eleanor Dixon.

Malory shortened her reins. "Good luck!" she called over her shoulder to Dylan.

"Back at you," Dylan replied.

Malory watched Bluegrass follow Skylark and Shamrock into the arena, and sent Hardy after them. They trotted into the center and halted. Malory noticed a quick flash of a hand waving from the front row of bleachers. Two alumnae were looking straight at Lynsey. *They must be part of the famous Team Harrison,* Malory realized. She swallowed nervously. *I wonder if Lynsey's told them all about the scholarship girl who's never ridden the top show circuit.*

As if he was picking up on her sudden change in mood, Hardy swung his quarters sideways, and Malory concentrated on keeping him still while Lynsey broke away from the group to jump first.

From the moment she and Bluegrass cleared the red-and-white rails, they were perfect. Halfway around the course, when Bluegrass sailed over the wall, the audience burst into applause.

Malory glanced sideways at Dylan. "She makes it look so easy," she whispered.

Dylan nodded. "She sure is keeping up the Harrison track record."

Bluegrass snapped up his forelegs to clear the first of the combination fences. He put in a bounce stride before sailing over the second fence. Lynsey patted his neck and cantered him back to the group, a wide smile on her face.

Dylan was up next. Malory's fingers tightened on the reins, making Hardy fidget. "Go clear, go clear," she muttered as she watched her friend fly over the first fence.

Four strides out from the wall, Morello laid back his ears as if he didn't like the look of the bright red wooden blocks. Dylan gave him a light tap with her crop, and Morello launched into the air with a snort. Malory held her breath as the gelding only just cleared the wall, rattling the top row of blocks with his hind legs. They jumped the spread and the vertical without difficulty and then turned into the corner. Malory watched Dylan slow the gelding and counted Morello's strides, *one, two, three*, as Dylan pointed him toward the combination. The paint gelding stood well back and sprang into the air to clear the first fence. Like Bluegrass, he put in one short stride to sail over the second jump. They were clear!

Malory wanted to cheer along with everyone else after Dylan's solid finish, but it was her turn to jump. She scooped up the reins, trying not to think about the hundreds of eyes trained on her. *Please, please let me go clear,* she begged. It was her first official course after making the competition team, and she didn't want to let the other riders down. Even more, she wanted to avoid being the target of Lynsey Harrison's petty taunts.

Hardy snatched at the reins as they cantered toward the red-and-white poles. "Steady," Malory whispered, holding her legs against him to maintain his bouncy stride but keeping a firm rein so that he wouldn't rush and flatten over the fence. Three yards away, she pushed her hands forward and let him take a fast, powerful stride before the jump. *Go, boy!* she thought as Hardy launched into the air.

The next two fences flashed past, and then they were cantering toward the parallel bars. Hardy listened to Malory right until he took off, forming a beautiful rounded arc over the fence. Malory felt a thrill of delight as she turned him to face the upright. *All of our practice has really paid off!* She relaxed a little as she judged the distance to their takeoff.

The next thing Malory knew, Hardy's nose was in the air, and they were going too fast on the approach. When Hardy took the jump, he lost the graceful outline he had had over the previous fence. His forelegs knocked against the pole, making it bounce in its holders. *Please stay up,* Malory prayed, not daring to look back and risk losing Hardy's focus again. The crowd groaned as the pole thudded onto the sand, and Malory felt her stomach drop with disappointment. She bit her lip and put a hundred and ten percent concentration into getting over the remaining jumps.

When Hardy landed clear over the final fence, the crowd burst into applause that was just as loud as for Dylan's and Lynsey's rounds, but that didn't make

Malory feel any better. She cantered back to the group, staring down at Hardy's mane. As far as she was concerned, she'd let the entire team down. It was not the ride the audience would have expected of the prestigious Rockwell grant recipient.

"Good job," Eleanor mouthed.

Malory gave a half smile.

"That was great," Dylan whispered when Malory halted alongside her.

Malory watched Olivia fly around the course on Shamrock. The dark gray mare pricked her ears as they raced toward the wall. "I feel like such an idiot for losing my concentration before the upright," she muttered.

"I think you're being too hard on yourself," Dylan replied. "I bet everyone in this arena thinks you did really well."

Malory couldn't help shooting a glance at the other team riders. *As long as Lynsey is around, there is no way Dylan would win that bet.*

🐾

Malory led Hardy into his stall, still feeling mad at herself for the dropped pole. Every other member of the team had gone clear. She listened to the running commentary Dylan was giving Morello in the next box stall. "You're going to get a treat tonight, boy. In fact, I might

snag some apples from the dinner buffet. Or some carrot cake."

Malory rubbed Hardy's nose. *I hope Diane Rockwell wasn't
here,* she thought, slipping the bridle over his ears. She
didn't want to think that her scholarship might be in
jeopardy if she didn't start turning in clear rounds.
Suddenly Hardy lifted his head and looked past her. The
sound of lively voices came down the aisle, and two tall
young women looked over the half-door.

"You're Malory O'Neil, right?" said one of them. Her
shining blonde hair was cut into neat bangs that swept
stylishly over her forehead, and her green eyes were
friendly as she smiled at Malory.

"That's me," Malory said, her brain whirring as she
tried to place the alumnae, who somehow looked familiar.
Maybe she had seen them in one of the Chestnut Hill
riding brochures?

"I'm Rachel, and this is Sienna," the girl explained,
placing a hand on the shoulder of her companion. *Lynsey's
sisters!* With a jolt Malory realized why they looked so
familiar; they had the same sleek blonde hair and high
cheekbones, although Lynsey's eyes were a smoky blue,
not green.

"We just wanted to congratulate you on your round,"
Rachel told her warmly. "You were great. I've never seen
Hardy jump like that. He's been here since before I came

to Chestnut Hill, and he was always so stubborn. But he looked like a champion out there, and I know he is a tricky pony to figure out."

Malory blinked. *Are you guys really related to Lynsey?* she wanted to ask. There was no way her classmate would have given her an ounce of credit for her riding today. "Thanks," she said, feeling her cheeks turn pink. "I just wish we'd gone clear! Hardy jumped his heart out, but I lost my concentration before that one fence."

"No worries." Sienna grinned. "It's still early in the year. I didn't ride here — I was on the tennis and field hockey teams — but even I can tell that it takes real talent to get this pony to look as good as he did. You two are quite a team. He'd jump mountains for you."

Malory was a little overwhelmed. It was clear that the sisters were going out of their way to be supportive of her. She was trying to think of a gracious reply when she saw Lynsey walking down the aisle.

"Well, I'll be around to see Lynsey at some of the shows," Rachel said. "I'll be on the lookout for you, Malory. I think you and Hardy could have quite a year."

"And don't beat yourself up over knocking down a single pole," Rachel added. "It happens to the best of us."

Lynsey paused in front of the chestnut's stall. Her face was unreadable as she squeezed between her sisters to stand at the door. She swept her eyes over Hardy, who was nosing his empty hay net. Then to Malory's astonishment, Lynsey turned to her and beamed. "I absolutely agree. Really, Malory, you should be proud of what you've done with Hardy. It's amazing he only knocked down one pole. It's not as if he has champion bloodlines or anything."

Malory froze. She had a feeling that Lynsey wasn't talking about horses. She was cutting on Malory's background.

Malory heard a stall door slap shut, and she saw Dylan appear next to the Harrisons, her cheeks flushed. It was obvious she had understood Lynsey's loaded comment. "I don't think that *pedigree* guarantees anything," she said, rubbing the bristles of a brisk brush against her palm.

Malory's heart sped up. The last thing she wanted was for Dylan and Lynsey to hit full stride in one of their insult-swapping spats, especially when Rachel and Sienna seemed so nice. Malory flashed her eyes at Dylan, but her friend played the oblivious card.

"What do you think, Rachel?" Dylan inquired. "How important is a good pedigree?"

Rachel paused. "Well, breeding is a strong indicator of potential; but I feel a horse's heart is his most valuable asset, and I don't think bloodlines can predict that."

Before Dylan could respond, Lynsey spoke up. "If you're done looking at Hardy, why don't you come over to see Blue? You need to congratulate him on his clear round."

Malory took a deep breath. Of course Lynsey would remind them all that Bluegrass had been perfect. *But Lynsey's sisters thought I rode well. And coming from a former senior riding team captain, that's worth a lot — more than a week's worth of Lynsey's insults!*

CHAPTER FOUR

I've died and gone to heaven." Dylan stopped abruptly halfway across the Adams sitting room and grabbed Malory's arm. "There must be fifty different dishes here."

Malory smiled. Dylan's passion for food was becoming legendary. "Even you couldn't sample everything." She ran her eyes over the tables that had been set out along the far wall. There were bowls piled high with all the classic favorites — nachos, chips, cheesecake, slices of pizza. . . .

She glanced back to Dylan, but her friend had vanished.

Lani wandered up with a loaded plate. "If you're looking for Dylan, I just saw her take a dive into the potato salad. I think it'll be a while before she resurfaces. I just hope she doesn't drown in the mayo."

Malory laughed. "I'll grab some pizza and wait it out." She helped herself to a soda first, then she practically had to fight her way out of the crowd of girls around the table before making her way toward her classmates' favorite group of sofas. She sat down opposite Lani, who was squeezed between Razina and Wei Lin.

"Is that all you're having?" Wei Lin asked.

Malory glanced down at her one slice of pizza. She wasn't very hungry. She was still frustrated with herself for knocking down the upright, and she had a hard time eating when she was emotionally out of sync.

"You were great today," Razina said, her dark eyes alight with enthusiasm. "You guys certainly represented Adams House well!"

"Yes, we were almost perfect," Lynsey said meaningfully as she joined them along with Patience. She put her plate down on the coffee table and flashed Malory a smile. "Kind of a shocker that it was the scholarship girl who sent the pole flying."

Malory felt her cheeks burn. She knew that despite the smile, Lynsey was sharpening her claws.

"Get over it, Lynsey," Lani told her.

"I'm sure Lynsey didn't mean it the way it sounded," Razina spoke up. "The whole team gave a stellar performance. Almost enough to make me want to get into the saddle."

"Hey, you know you can take riding as an elective," Lani said encouragingly, turning to Razina.

Malory was grateful for Razina's and Lani's enthusiasm,

especially since it took the attention off Lynsey's assessment of her and Hardy's ride that day.

"Scoot over." Dylan broke in on her thoughts, and Malory looked up to see her friend juggling two plates heavy with food.

Lynsey raised her eyebrows. "Oh, it's so cute that you got enough to share with Morello, but I'm not sure your aunt would approve of him eating all that stuff. It might be too much — even for a horse." She lifted a forkful of mixed salad.

Malory was sure Dylan would have had a comeback, but she had a forkful of macaroni and cheese in her mouth.

"What's Lucy pinning on the notice board?" asked Alexandra Cooper, looking over at the board near the door.

Malory narrowed her eyes to see what Lucy Weisbin, a student council representative, was doing. "I think it's a poster for the Halloween party," she said, when Lucy stood back to reveal a poster with a striking border of black cats.

"Cool!" Lynsey sounded unusually enthusiastic. "I hope they're doing it all properly. When I helped organize my school's Halloween party last year, we hired this amazing theatrical company my mom uses for decorating her events. I wonder if the student council would like their number."

"This isn't a benefit ball, you know," Dylan said.

"Since I'm not intellectually challenged, yes I do," Lynsey replied with saccharin dripping from her voice.

"Have you guys decided what you're wearing next Saturday?" Wei Lin asked.

"Still working on it," Dylan told her. "What about you?"

"Razina and I got our costumes in town last week," Wei Lin said. "We have a tennis match next Saturday so it was our only chance."

Malory leaned forward. "What did you get?" She knew everyone was buzzing about the forthcoming Halloween party, but she'd hardly given it a second's thought, she'd been so preoccupied with the practice for the exhibition.

"I cheated, really," Razina confessed. "I had my mom send the dress I wore when I played Tallulah in *Bugsy Malone* at my last school. I just bought some extras to liven it up."

"Oh, I've always wanted to dance in one of those flapper dresses!" Honey exclaimed. "I'm so jealous."

Razina laughed. "As much as I love you, I'm not taking it off on the dance floor for you to have a turn."

"That would certainly be a hearty welcome for the Saint Kits boys," Dylan said, her eyes sparkling.

Malory blinked. She'd forgotten that boys from their brother school would be coming to the dance. She instantly thought of Caleb, the dark-haired boy whom she'd met at her stable over the summer. She knew he went to Saint Kits, but they hadn't been in touch since the start of the term, even though she'd seen him at a joint-school symposium. She hadn't said hello then, partially because all the girls were making a big deal about the boys, and Malory wasn't really into that. Besides, she wouldn't have known what to say. It had been so easy at the stable because they could always talk about horses.

"Do you think any of the boys will call us and ask us to go with them?" Patience asked.

"It's not a prom!" Dylan protested. "One, they don't have any of our numbers, and two, most of them don't even know our names."

Malory glanced up to see Lynsey and Patience exchange a loaded glance. *What are they hiding?*

"And three, they'll have plenty of time to hit on us when they arrive!" Dylan finished with a broad grin. "I'd much rather have my options open than be stuck with one dance partner all night."

Malory laughed along with the others, trying to look forward to the dance without thinking about Caleb. But Malory knew she had told Dylan about him, and she wouldn't put it past her friend to try some totally unsubtle matchmaking.

"What are you wearing, Wei Lin?" Alexandra asked when they had quieted down.

"I'll give you a clue." Wei Lin put her plate down on

the table and stood up. Keeping her feet close together, she folded her arms and shuffled forward awkwardly.

Patience frowned. "You're going as a *mummy*?"

"My guess is Morticia Addams," Lani said.

"And the prize goes to Lani Hernandez." Wei Lin pulled a mock bow before collapsing back down on the sofa.

"Since when does Morticia Addams shuffle when she walks?" Lynsey said.

"That wasn't shuffling!" Wei Lin pretended to look affronted. "That was sashaying. But," she hesitated, "I promise it will look better when I have my costume on."

"What are the two of you going as?" Honey addressed Lynsey and Patience.

"Don't even try," Razina interrupted. "Apparently their outfits are top secret."

"You know, we'd tell you but then we'd have to kill you." Lynsey rattled off the old line without a hint of humor. She dabbed at the corner of her mouth with a napkin and turned to Malory and Dylan. "You guys haven't forgotten that we have to pick up our junior team fleeces on Monday?" She glanced sideways at Malory with a fake sympathetic smile. "That's when we'll be fitted for our formal jackets as well. It certainly isn't cheap to be on the competition team. I don't know how I'd manage without my dad's gold card."

Malory felt her stomach flip over. She'd forgotten they had to pick up the fleeces this week. *And we'll probably have to pay for the fitted jacket in advance,* she thought. *I'll never be able to pay for that and a costume out of my allowance.* The scholarship paid for her tuition and board, but there were often unexpected fees for supplies and field trips. Her dad sent her an allowance each month, and Malory almost always had some left over, but there wouldn't be enough to cover this kind of expense.

"Of course, I'm sure Ms. Carmichael must have some secondhand uniforms lying around for girls who don't want their own or can't afford it." Lynsey stretched out her hand and examined her French-manicured nails.

Patience rolled her eyes and gave Lynsey a playful slap on the arm. *They deserve each other*, Malory thought.

The thought of asking Ms. Carmichael for a second-hand fleece and formal jacket had occurred to her, but after Lynsey's snide remark, she'd make sure she bought a new one even if it took every penny of her allowance. "Just because I don't have a gold card doesn't mean I can't pay my own way," she said. "I prefer cash anyway."

She felt Dylan looking at her with a combination of admiration and concern, but right now she didn't want to acknowledge either. *How am I ever going to fit in if Lynsey keeps making a big thing out of money?* Malory took in a deep breath. "My dad brought me up to believe that it's rude to discuss money in public, so maybe we can get back to a more civilized conversation?"

A hush fell over the group until Lani spoke up. "I think we can declare Malory the winner of *that* round."

Lynsey turned her back and bent her head close to Patience's. Malory sighed. *What do you bet they're already plotting how to get me back?* Malory knew she had made some good friends at Chestnut Hill — she just wished she hadn't made enemies as well.

🐾

Malory carefully hung up the navy-blue fleece with the Chestnut Hill logo embroidered on one side. Right now she didn't care that she had invested every cent of this month's allowance on riding gear. In just over four weeks, she'd be wearing the fleece for their first official team competition! Six teams from local schools were going to be competing at Saint Kits in what had been billed as a friendly warm-up for the All Schools League, but which was starting to feel like the first round of the World Cup. Because it was an unofficial meet, they could wear their warm-up fleeces rather than their formal attire, which wouldn't arrive from the tailor until after Thanksgiving.

Dylan stuck her head around the door. "Hey, Mal. Are you coming down to the common room? Lani and Honey want to brainstorm ideas about costumes for the Halloween party."

Malory's heart plummeted. She didn't know how she

would manage to pull together a costume without any money or seamstress savvy.

She trailed down to the sitting room with Dylan sympathizing about their riding lesson earlier that day. Ms. Carmichael had asked everyone to ride a different pony, and Malory had ended up on Soda, who had proven to be a bit of a bear. "I heard that Emily Page rode Soda in a jumping class before ours, and this morning he was used in a senior sidesaddle class," Dylan explained. "He must have been pretty worn out by the time you got around to riding him."

Malory smiled. It was so typical of Dylan to try to make her feel better. "You looked good on Shamrock," she said. It was the first time that Dylan had ridden the pretty Irish-bred mare.

"She's nice," Dylan agreed. "But I'm happy to let Olivia Buckley ride her on the team, though. There's no way I'm swapping Morello for anything!"

Malory felt relieved she'd managed to disguise her worries from her friend.

Honey was sitting cross-legged on one of the sofas, chewing the end of a pencil as she and Lani studied a pile of sketches on the coffee table.

Dylan leaned over the back of the sofa. "Did Mr. Woolley give out an art assignment without me noticing?"

"No, we decided to draw some of our costume design ideas," Honey told her.

"That's a great idea," Dylan said, her eyes lighting up. "Have you got a spare pencil?"

"Help yourself," Lani said, rolling one across the table.

Dylan swung her legs over the sofa and slid down between Honey and Lani. She picked up a spare sheet of paper and began to sketch what looked to be a cross between Scooby-Doo and Big Foot. "What do you think, Mal?"

"I think it might need a bit more work." Malory laughed, sitting down on the opposite sofa. She pulled across some of the designs. "Hey, these are really good!" She held up an outline of a fringed cowboy jacket and matching full-length chaps. "Annie Oakley?"

"Close." Lani smiled. "I was thinking more along the lines of the Lone Ranger."

"Cool," Malory said. She looked at a second sketch of a kilt and laced sandals. "Wow — Peter Pan."

Honey shook her head. "Actually it's Robin Hood." She grinned. "Robbing from the rich and all that." She pulled out an imaginary arrow from behind her shoulder, aimed, and fired. Malory pretended to duck.

"Lynsey and Patience had better watch out!" Lani said.

"Where are they anyway?" Dylan asked, looking around the sitting room. "This whole place seems deserted."

"Lynsey's off campaigning for student council," Honey explained.

"And she's taken Patience, Wei Lin, and Razina with her to spread the word," Lani added.

Malory rolled her eyes. The instant Lynsey had decided to run for student council, she had become a living, breathing infomercial for herself. Her platform seemed to revolve around amping up the social calendar.

"So Mal, have you decided what you're wearing yet?" Lani asked.

Even though an image of someone draped in a white sheet with holes cut into it flashed in her mind, she refused to answer ghost. "I'm still working on it," she stalled, rolling a pencil under her fingers.

"Well, I hope you've got it figured out by Saturday." Lani grinned wolfishly under her brown bangs. "This is one event you can't miss!"

Malory bit into an apple and watched a group of seniors set a picnic blanket close by the fountain. She and the others had chosen a shadier patch of lawn to picnic on, under a spreading sycamore tree. Even though it was Friday, everyone had been given the afternoon off in return for giving up the previous Saturday to help with Homecoming. Malory had been stressed for three days before and after the riding demonstration, but it still seemed like a good exchange!

"Throw me one of those apples, Mal," Lani said.

Malory tossed a red apple and grinned as Lani's hand shot up and neatly snagged it from the air even though Malory's throw was off by a mile. "Good catch," she said. "You remind me of my grandparents' dog."

"Gee thanks, Mal," Lani answered. "That's the kind of comment I'd expect from Lynsey."

"No! It was a compliment. I swear." Malory tried to salvage the conversation. "Really, Lani. I loved that dog."

"I didn't know your grandparents have a dog." Dylan rolled over onto her stomach and reached for her third Oreo.

"They don't now," Malory said, plucking a daisy and twirling it between her thumb and finger. Talking about herself was far from her favorite thing to do. "Max died the summer before they sold their farm and retired to the town."

"Oh, great!" Lani exclaimed. "Not only do I remind you of some mutt; it's a dead mutt."

"No, no, no. You've got it all wrong. Max wasn't a mutt, he was a black Lab." Now Malory was having fun with this, and she watched as Lani rolled her big, brown eyes.

"Labs are not supposed to be the smartest dogs in the world, you know," Lani advised.

"But they're loyal," said Dylan.

"Oh, well, that's me, all right," Lani agreed.

"Okay, okay. Let me explain," Malory said. "It's just

that Max was super playful, and he could snatch any ball from the air, even one thrown in the opposite direction of where he was running. And he did these great somersaults."

"It *is* you!" Honey declared, giving Lani an affectionate slap on the knee. "At least Max was a cool dog, not some hairless lap pup."

"Max was the best," Malory agreed.

"So did you spend a lot of time with your grandparents?" Dylan asked.

Malory nodded. "Every vacation Mom would take me there and spend a few days before heading back to help Dad with the business. I stayed for a few weeks at a time."

She lay back on the blanket, closing her eyes as she pictured her mom weeding her grandparents' backyard, pestered by a plump, scarlet-feathered chicken that kept weaving in and out of her feet. "Oh, Martha," she said aloud.

"Who?" Dylan prompted.

"Martha — she was this huge red hen my mom raised from a chick. Whenever she visited, Martha would follow her everywhere — even into the house! Then when my mom headed back to town, Martha would start to follow me."

"It sounds like your mom was pretty cool," Honey said softly.

"She was the greatest. She had this whole connection with animals. She seemed to know what they were thinking, and I never saw one that didn't totally trust her."

"Like Dr. Dolittle," Lani said.

"Pretty much." Malory laughed.

"And now you have the gift," Dylan put in.

Malory shifted uncomfortably. She didn't think she could communicate with animals on the same level as her mom — but she knew her mom wouldn't agree. She had called Malory a natural when she had found her sitting astride a neighbor's dark brown quarterhorse gelding with no saddle or bridle. Malory had been only six years old, but scrambling off the top of the gate onto Zanzibar's back seemed like the most natural thing in the world.

"Did your grandparents have any horses?" Honey asked.

"No, but I used to spend hours hanging around the neighbor's horse. His pasture was just outside my bedroom window, and I used to dream that he was mine. He was a beautiful quarterhorse named Zanzibar." Malory gave a dramatic sigh. "He was my first-ever equine crush!" she joked, letting humor hide how much effort it took to reveal these memories. "His owners used to let me ride him bareback around the field and didn't tell Mom when I fell off over and over. But it didn't take her long to figure out that I was addicted." Malory smiled.

Even though she slid off easily as he trotted around the field, Zanzibar always seemed to want her to get back on, patiently waiting as she attempted to mount with a running vault. One morning after her mom had witnessed at least ten falls, Malory was certain she would be banned from riding Zan. Instead, her mom put her arm around Malory's shoulder and promised that she would arrange for her to take proper riding lessons — with actual tack — at the local stables back home.

Malory couldn't believe her mom would never look at her that way again. Even though her mom had never been interested in riding herself, the day Malory arrived home from her grandparents' that summer, they headed for Cheney Falls Stables. She was only eight but she knew that riding lesson had changed her life.

Dylan stood up and brushed crumbs off her jeans. "Well, on that note, I think I owe my folks an e-mail. I'm going to the computer lab in the student center. Any takers?"

Jolted from her reverie, Malory grabbed her messenger bag. "I'll come with you." She wanted to send some pictures to her dad. Lani had snapped a great shot of her and Hardy clearing the combination at Homecoming.

"Later," Honey and Lani called as Malory and Dylan headed over the lawn.

"See you, Honey. See you, *Max*!" Dylan yelled back.

Lani scrunched up her nose and narrowed her eyes at

her friends, and Malory grinned sheepishly. She did have wonderful memories of Max and all the days spent on her grandparents' farm. They almost seemed like they belonged to another lifetime.

🦬

After sending their e-mails, the girls headed over to the stables. As they walked across the yard, they saw Ms. Carmichael sitting in her SUV with the trailer hooked up behind. She leaned out of the window and waved. "Hey! I'm going to check out some ponies for sale on the other side of town. Do you want to come with me?"

The girls glanced at each other in excitement. "Of course!" they answered in unison.

CHAPTER FIVE

So how many horses are we buying?" Dylan asked, leaning forward so her aunt could see her in the Jeep's rearview mirror.

"Only two!" Ms. Carmichael replied. "And that's providing they turn out to be as good as the dealer promised." She slowed down before pulling onto the main road. "How would you guys feel about riding them for me? I'll need to see how they go, and I might be too long in the leg to get a good sense."

"I'm all for it!" Malory confirmed, catching Dylan's eye. *What could be better than getting to try out new horses?*

The drive across town took thirty minutes through busy end-of-week traffic, and Malory was tingling with apprehension by the time Ms. Carmichael pulled into the parking lot at the front of an impressive-looking yard. Malory and Dylan scrambled out before the engine tapered out.

On the drive over, Ali had explained that the yard mainly imported Sport Horses, although the horses they were looking at today had come from a local auction.

Malory looked around, breathing in the delicious smells of hay and horses. The yard reminded her of the stables at Cheney Falls where she had ridden before. The layout was so similar she half expected to see Elaine, her riding instructor, walk around the corner leading Apollo, the lanky chestnut who was a favorite with all the riders. Malory sighed; even Apollo couldn't replace Zanzibar in her affections. The dark brown quarterhorse she'd learned to ride on would always be number one for her.

As Malory and Dylan followed Ms. Carmichael across the yard to the office, a tall man with gray-flecked dark hair stepped out. "Ms. Carmichael, glad you could make it," he greeted her.

"Good afternoon, Mr. Ryan. These are two of my junior-team riders." Ms. Carmichael introduced Malory and Dylan. "They're going to try the horses out for me."

"Great." The manager smiled. "I've left them in the paddock for you." He gestured to a path behind the stable block. "It's just down there. I thought you'd like to see how they are at being caught and tacked up."

Malory nodded approvingly. *That's a good start. He's obviously confident about the ponies' personalities.*

She and Dylan headed up the path, with Mr. Ryan

and Ms. Carmichael following behind. The path widened into a track that led to a white-railed paddock. Malory shaded her eyes from the sun, studying the horses they were going to be trying out. The one nearest to her was a showy bright bay mare; a gray cob gelding grazed beside her, swishing his tail. Malory guessed that the gelding was fifteen hands and the mare about a hand smaller. "What are their names?" she asked Mr. Ryan.

"The bay is Foxy Lady, and the gray is Winter Wonderland, otherwise known as Winnie." Mr. Ryan pulled back the clasp on the wooden gate and handed the girls two halters he had brought with him. "Help yourselves, girls. Use the first two stalls in the barn. Their tack will be in the tack room at the end of the aisle." He pushed the gate open. "Bring them down to the exercise paddock when you're ready."

Malory grinned at Dylan as they walked through the gateway.

"Which one do you want?" Dylan asked.

"It looks like they've already chosen," Malory pointed out as the gray stretched out to sniff Dylan.

Malory walked up to the mare, who was watching her with her small ears pricked forward. "Hello, gorgeous," she said softly. She rubbed Foxy Lady's nose and then slipped the halter on. It was obvious from the mare's dished face that she had Arabian blood, which was going to make her a lively ride.

Dylan led Winnie, and together they walked the horses into the cool barn.

"What do you bet this one has all kinds of hang-ups?" Dylan called as she disappeared into the first stall.

"Huh?" Malory frowned, leading Foxy Lady into the adjoining stall.

"It can't be easy being a boy called Winnie," Dylan pointed out.

"Serves you right if he decides to throw you," Malory joked, slipping out of the stall to fetch the tack. "He might not like having everyone's attention drawn to it!"

"You are so harsh," Dylan pretended to complain.

The smell of leather hit Malory as she stepped into the tack room. So many rows of saddles and bridles lined the walls that it took her a while until she spotted Foxy Lady's name scribbled on a chalkboard under some Havana-colored tack.

She scooped it up and placed it on Foxy Lady's door. Even though the mare's coat looked pretty clean, she wanted to give her a quick going-over with a body brush before she tacked her up. "I don't want any hidden grains of dirt making you itch once I'm onboard," she told the mare. "I figure you're going to be enough of a live wire as it is." Foxy Lady snorted and scraped her hoof as if she was agreeing with Malory's rapid-fire character judgment. Malory smiled and began to draw a body brush over the mare's silky coat.

Ten minutes later she rode Foxy Lady into the sand arena. Winter Wonderland gave a loud snort behind her.

"Steady!" Dylan sounded amused. "You'll get to canter soon enough."

"Just work them through their paces," Ms. Carmichael called from where she was sitting on the fence next to Mr. Ryan.

When Malory asked Foxy Lady to trot, the mare gave a small buck as if she wanted to show she wasn't a pushover. Malory sat deeper into the saddle and brought Foxy Lady's hocks back underneath her. The mare snatched at the bit, but Malory changed the rein across the diagonal to keep her mind occupied. *I'll just keep you busy so you can't think up any stunts to pull on me!*

Out of the corner of her eye, she saw Dylan trotting Winnie on a fifteen-yard circle. The gelding looked relaxed and was bending nicely around Dylan's inside leg. Malory returned to the outside of the ring and clicked to Foxy Lady. The mare immediately lengthened her stride and snorted as if she had been waiting to show off her faster paces.

Wow, I'd like to see you and Lani go a round against the clock. Malory thought what a speed demon Lani was for timed jumping rounds. Foxy grudgingly slowed down to a collected canter, but Malory sensed she was just waiting for the chance to be given her head.

She kept her on a twenty-yard circle until Ms.

Carmichael cupped her hands and called, "Take them into the jumping arena now."

Malory followed Dylan into the next paddock and halted Foxy Lady just inside the gate. The mare swung her quarters out, and Malory missed seeing Dylan take the first of the six jumps. There was a dull thud, and she looked up to see a blue-and-white pole lying on the ground. Dylan was urging Winnie on to the second jump, her face set with determination, and the gray gelding carefully popped over the cross pole. The next jump was an upright, and Winnie slowed his pace. Dylan tapped him with her whip one stride too late, and Winnie knocked the top bar with his forelegs as he took off.

Malory winced; Winnie was very sweet — and obviously didn't bear any grudges about his name — but he wasn't going to make any of the jumping teams!

Dylan finished the course with two more lackluster jumps. She rubbed his neck as she trotted back to Malory. "He's trying, but I don't think he's got much spring to him!"

Malory grinned and sent Foxy Lady forward. The mare shot at the first jump, and Malory found herself concentrating more on holding her back than on trying to see her stride. "Steady!" A shower of sand flew up into the air from the mare's hooves as they launched over the fence. There was a second of silence, and then they landed and were racing toward the second.

Foxy Lady cleared every fence and gave a buck when she completed the course. Malory let the mare gallop down the length of the ring before slowing her. *That was amazing!*

"I guess you like her," Dylan smiled as Malory leaned forward and patted Foxy Lady's damp neck.

"She's an incredible jumper," Malory agreed, straightening up.

Ms. Carmichael walked over to join them in the center of the paddock. "They both went well for you," she said, "although Foxy will need a lot of work to help her realize that there are speeds other than fast!"

"Winnie's really responsive on the flat. I can see another dressage pro in the making," Dylan chipped in.

"Thank you, Dylan," said Ms. Carmichael. "So do you both think they will make good additions to the Chestnut Hill stable?"

"I don't think Foxy would be suitable for beginners, but she'll fit in perfectly for the intermediate group. We should team her up with Lani against the clock. I reckon they'd be unbeatable," Malory said.

"Okay, take them back to the barn and untack them. I'll get back to Mr. Ryan and try some haggling over prices," Ms. Carmichael said.

Once Malory had hung up her tack, she went to the adjoining stall and looked over the door. "Do you want a hand?"

"I'm just about done, thanks," Dylan said, sponging Winnie's ears.

Malory decided to head down the aisle to see if there were any other horses around. Most of the stalls were empty, but as she got closer to the end of the barn, a palomino pony looked out over her door.

"Hello there," Malory murmured, holding out her hand for the pony to smell.

The palomino brushed her lips over Malory's palm and then moved back to the hay rack on the opposite wall.

Two stalls down, a beautiful gray Warmblood stuck his head out at the sound of Malory's voice. *Wow!* She hurried over to admire the handsome horse — and stopped dead.

There was a pony standing in the shadows at the back of the stall between the palomino and the gray. His small, neat head, slender legs, and the glossy dark brown of his coat looked so familiar that for a moment Malory couldn't breathe.

"Zan?" she whispered. The dark brown horse turned to look at her, and she flinched away. This horse wasn't Zanzibar. There was no way he would ever have looked so wary and mistrustful.

But he looked so like Malory's beloved quarterhorse that she still felt drawn to him. She stepped up to the stall and took a breath. "Hey, gorgeous." She held out her hand.

The pony flattened his ears and didn't move from the back corner. Malory's heart twisted with pity. Zanzibar had been totally trusting and affectionate, even when Malory had been only six years old.

She leaned her arms on the stable door and thought back to how devastated she had been when her grandparents had decided to sell their farm. The peaceful wooden house, with its wraparound deck and old porch swing, had always been like a second home to her. On top of leaving the comfort and freedom she felt there, she had had to say good-bye to Zan. He had felt like part of her family.

The dark horse pawed at the ground, the tip of his hoof scraping through the straw to drag across the concrete underneath. The raw sound made Malory shudder. He seemed unhappy and caught up in his own fears, but Malory could not bring herself to believe that a horse so similar to Zanzibar could be so different. She slid back the bolt, and the pony threw up his head, tossing his jet-black mane.

Malory gasped and grabbed the door frame. There was a small whorl of hair on the pony's neck, just below the line of his mane. Zanzibar had had exactly the same mark, in the exact same place. It was a totally natural, but very unusual, quirk of hair growth. According to superstition, it was a sign that the horse was very special.

Malory wasn't sure if she was being brave or stupid as

she walked across the stall. The pony rolled his eyes, flashing the whites. "Easy, I'm not going to hurt you." *He's so nervous*, Malory thought. *I wonder what happened to him.*

Now she was closer and could see that his breeding was different than that of Zanzibar. Even though his coat wasn't as sleek and well-groomed as the other horses at the stable, his elegant legs and well-muscled hind-quarters looked a lot like an English Thoroughbred. His height suggested that he had pony ancestry as well, perhaps even quarterhorse like Zan. Despite his wary posture, there was something decidedly noble about his handsome head and wide-set eyes. Just like Zanzibar, his coat was a dark chocolate brown — and he had the slightest sliver of a star on his forehead.

"What's your story, fella?" she said softly. She raised her hand once more for the pony to sniff and then bent her head down to blow gently into his nostrils — the way horses greet each other. The pony froze, and Malory thought he was going to jerk away from her. But then to her relief, he blew back. It was the first step toward becoming friends!

"What are you up to?" Dylan appeared at the door. The gelding laid back his ears and swished his tail. "Whoa, he looks kind of mean."

"I think he's more nervous than mean," Malory defended him. She moved quickly back to the door when she saw that Mr. Ryan and Ms. Carmichael were with Dylan. She hoped she wasn't going to get into trouble for going into the pony's stall.

"I agree with your character assessment," said Mr. Ryan, looking serious. "We just bought Tybalt a few days ago, which is why he's not quite as groomed or conditioned as our other horses. He was going real cheap in the auction, but he could really move. We thought with some schooling he might turn into a good prospect." He turned to Ms. Carmichael. "If you have a student willing to give him some extra time, I think you'd be happy with the results."

Malory brightened and looked at Ms. Carmichael. *I'm game,* she thought.

But the expression on Ms. Carmichael's face was far from promising. She seemed to be giving Tybalt a very critical review.

"I don't know. I had only planned on adding two horses at this time, and he doesn't seem nearly as adjusted as the other two." She gave her watch a glance. "I don't really have time to watch him go now, either. We need to get the other two back."

"Well, I understand your hesitation," Mr. Ryan said. "But I am prepared to make you a deal. I just bought two yearlings, and I'm going to have my hands full. I won't have much left for this fellow. I'll sell him to you for what I paid."

Malory looked at Tybalt, who lingered in the far corner of the stall as the two adults went back and forth.

"Maybe I can come back some other time," Ms. Carmichael said. "I can't put money down without seeing how he goes with a rider."

Malory knew Ms. Carmichael was doing sound business but wished she'd take the chance on Tybalt. Malory had a feeling that this horse was special. Beyond the whorl and his likeness to Zanzibar, Malory saw something in him. She couldn't put her finger on it, but she had to believe her instinct was right.

"I don't think he'll be here long, not if I advertise him at the price I paid," Mr. Ryan said.

Suddenly Mr. Ryan sounded more like a used-car salesman than a horse dealer. Under any other circumstances, Malory'd think he was just trying to get this horse off his lot.

Malory glanced at her teacher. Ms. Carmichael raised her eyebrows slightly when their eyes met, and Malory realized that it must be clear from her expression just how much she wanted this horse to come back with them. They couldn't leave Tybalt behind, they just couldn't!

CHAPTER SIX

Ms. Carmichael frowned. "Well, we do need more than two ponies," she said to Mr. Ryan, "but I'm not crazy about rushing into buying a third. Especially one who's nervy."

"Maybe he's just unsettled from being in a new home and all," Malory suggested. The more she studied the wary pony at the back of the stable, the more she felt convinced she could help him. It was the same feeling she'd had when she'd found an old tabby cat curled up in a pile of boxes in the alley behind her dad's store. Over several days she had gained his trust with pieces of fish. Eventually she and her mom had coaxed him inside and had given him the name Marmalade. They had spent hours sitting close to him beside the fire. Malory had not forced him to be held but had waited patiently until he had made up his mind that he wanted to be friends.

"Think about it if you want," Mr. Ryan said.

In the silence that followed, Ms. Carmichael narrowed her eyes.

"He's a good height," she admitted. "And he's obviously got good breeding."

"Look, why don't you take him on trial?" Mr. Ryan suggested. "If you're not happy with him after a month, I'll take him back and give you a full refund."

Malory held her breath. Ms. Carmichael's eyes scanned from the horse, to her scholarship student, to Mr. Ryan.

"You've got a deal," she declared, holding out her hand. She looked back at Malory. "I can tell you're smitten! Let's hope your instincts are right."

Malory looked back at Tybalt. She hoped she was right, too.

🐎

Malory waited for Dylan to lead Foxy Lady into the trailer and back her into the spot next to Winnie. Tybalt shifted his weight restlessly at the bottom of the ramp. "You'll be all right," Malory soothed. "See how easy it was for Winnie and Foxy?" She pulled on the lead rope, but Tybalt refused to move.

"Do you want a hand?" Mr. Ryan called.

Malory shook her head. She reached up to massage

Tybalt's neck in what she hoped was a decent imitation of the T-touch method that she had seen Amy Fleming do at the symposium. She hoped the veterinary student's alternative therapies would work on the anxious gelding. "Take all the time you want," she murmured. "I know you don't want to get into another trailer and go to another new home, but I promise there's a big bucket of feed waiting for you there, and lots of friends." She kept talking to Tybalt, but he remained rigid and unmoving. "I'll take care of you," she promised before trying to put pressure on the rope again. This time the dark gelding took a step onto the ramp. He paused one final time and then followed Malory all the way up.

"Way to go!" Dylan called, helping Ms. Carmichael and Mr. Ryan to lift the ramp.

Malory carefully tied Tybalt and gave him one last pat before ducking out through the side door. *Let's just hope his arrival at Chestnut Hill goes as smoothly.*

Can I put Tybalt in his stall?" Malory asked Ms. Carmichael when they arrived at Chestnut Hill.

"Sure. Dylan and I will take the others. You can put him in the box stall next to Rose," Ms. Carmichael told her. "You'll have to put straw down, though, since I wasn't expecting to come back with three horses!" She looked at

Dylan. "Winnie's going to the far stable block. I'll take him. But could you put Foxy in number six, please?"

"Sure," Dylan replied.

Tybalt unloaded first, and Malory didn't wait for the others. She wanted to get him settled right away. She led the gelding into the stall at the end of the aisle, smiling at the way he looked all around him, snorting at the strange smells. "There you go," she said, reaching up to unbuckle his halter.

He skittered away from her, his shoes clanging against the floor. Malory walked over and placed her hand on his neck. Tybalt shifted uneasily, but when she began to move her fingers in small circles again, he gave a sigh and lowered his head. Malory felt a small thrill of delight; whether she was doing T-touch right or not, it certainly seemed to help calm him.

"Good boy," she whispered as Tybalt half closed his eyes. She took comfort in the feel of him leaning his head against her. It was so familiar, it made her catch her breath. She had to remind herself she wasn't back on her grandparents' farm, and this wasn't Zanzibar.

Suddenly a horse clattered down the aisle. Tybalt's eyes flew open, and he backed into the corner, almost knocking Malory over. "Steady," she tried to soothe him. This was all the reminder she needed that he wasn't the steady, gentle quarterhorse she rode as a child.

Sarah stopped Rose by Tybalt's door and let out a

whistle as she admired the new arrival. "Take a look at him!"

"Yeah, he's easy on the eyes, isn't he?" Malory agreed. "But he's kind of wound up right now."

Sarah smiled. "Well, that's understandable. Let's hope he gets over that soon." She clicked to Rose to lead her into the adjoining stall. "I'll go get some straw if you want some help," she offered.

"That would be great," Malory replied. She turned back to Tybalt but the dark pony laid back his ears.

"Okay, I get the message. I'll get you that bucket of feed I promised." She slipped out of his stall and was securing the bolt when Dylan appeared.

"How does he like his new home?"

"He's a little spooked," Malory admitted.

"Well, if anyone can get him to settle in, it's you," Dylan said. "You have *the touch*." She wiggled her fingers in the air and hummed the theme to the old *X-Files*.

Malory grinned. She didn't mind Dylan teasing her about how much she wanted to use the methods Amy Fleming had told them about at the symposium on alternative equine medicine. She glanced back over Tybalt's door. He was watching her carefully from the back of the stall, his flanks rising with swift, shallow breaths. Sarah was right — he did need to get over his nervousness soon. There was no way Ms. Carmichael would keep him if he stayed this skiddish and high-strung.

❧

Malory put her tray down on the cafeteria table where the Adams underclassmen sat. She pulled out the chair beside Dylan before sprinkling some Parmesan cheese on her lasagna.

"That smells fantastic. Now I wish I'd gone for the lasagna," Dylan said, looking down at her fried chicken and mashed potatoes.

Malory laughed. "What's the difference? You'll end up eating off my plate anyway."

"Where did everyone else go?" Honey asked as she joined them, looking at the empty chairs.

"Lynsey probably still has them working overtime, handing out flyers — the elections are on Monday," Alexandra told her.

"There can't be a single person on campus who hasn't seen one of her flyers," Dylan groaned. "Can't she give it a rest? Everywhere I go I see pictures of Lynsey smiling down at me. It's like a bad horror movie, and I'm starting to get creeped out."

"Well, on that subject, Dylan said one of the new school horses is a little creepy," Lani said.

When Malory heard Lani's comment, she put her fork down and looked at Dylan. She could only guess that her friend had mentioned Tybalt's anxious nature in passing to Lani, but Malory couldn't help but take it personally.

"I didn't say that," Dylan replied quickly, shooting Malory a glance. "I just said that he was pretty nervous."

"Oh, come on," Lani said, unaware of the tension brewing between Dylan and Malory. "You said he was absolutely beautiful, but you had no clue what was going on in his head."

"Well, that's what we say about you, too," Dylan replied with a smirk in Lani's direction. She laughed as she took another bite of fried chicken, but then she looked at Malory again. Malory had a feeling Dylan knew what was going through her mind because her friend's expression changed. "Look," she said with a deep breath. "We can never guess what a horse we don't know is thinking, and we don't know anything about the history of a new horse, either. I thought Tybalt looked a little wary, but Malory likes this guy, and I know she'll help him figure himself out."

She was grateful for Dylan's faith in her, but admitting she wanted to be the one to connect with Tybalt meant assuming responsibility for him.

"Did you ride him?" Honey asked.

Malory shook her head. "We didn't have time," she answered. "I think Ms. Carmichael will want him to settle in first before she has anyone ride him."

"Well, Mal, it sounds like the perfect opportunity to use some of the famous Amy Fleming's techniques," Lani suggested, reaching across for the saltshaker.

"Maybe." Malory felt shy about admitting just how much she wanted to win Tybalt's trust.

She'd love to try the alternative methods that Amy Fleming had developed at Heartland, her family's horse sanctuary. She believed Tybalt could be just as loyal and understanding as Zanzibar. And when he wasn't aware that people were around, he had seemed calm. Watching him just move around his stall, Malory had sensed that he had an almost lyrical grace about him. It was just a brief moment before he noticed her and tensed up again, but Malory knew she would cling to it, knowing he had something special.

"Well, Malory's obviously got confidence in him, and she's our one and only scholarship girl." Lani winked.

"There's no arguing with that," Honey agreed.

Malory crossed her fingers underneath the table. She knew her friends were only trying to pay her a compliment, but they didn't seem to understand how much extra pressure they were putting on her. It wasn't just the importance of keeping Tybalt at Chestnut Hill; it was proving to everyone, including herself, that she really deserved the prestigious Rockwell Award.

Malory hadn't been able to believe her luck when

Diane Rockwell had approached her at one of the early shows at Cheney Falls Stable that summer. Malory hadn't noticed the tall red-haired woman before then — which was a good thing since she was already hot and flustered enough from the events of the day. She estimated that she'd run the distance of a marathon between taking ponies from the trailer to the stalls, the stalls to the practice ring, and the practice ring to the show rings. Not to mention the fact that the trainer had trusted her to help the younger children mount, adjusting a hundred pairs of stirrup leathers along the way. She'd even found herself acting as general diplomat to smooth over issues with the kids' competitive parents!

When it had finally been her turn to ride, she felt as if she'd already completed a three-day event; and she'd tried not to groan out loud when Elaine told her she'd have to ride the infamous Checkmate. Malory had trained on Apollo, but he'd come up lame the night before. Checkmate was one of the more temperamental characters at the stable, and he had already made a point of stating that it wasn't one of his better days. He'd refused a fence and then run out of the last class, giving a flying buck after his rider had tapped him with her crop.

"Earth to Malory. What are you thinking about?" Dylan nudged her.

Malory blinked. "Nothing much."

"Well, it looked like something. If I didn't know better I would have thought you were practicing telekinesis or something," Lani teased.

"Very funny! I only do that stuff in our room," Malory joked. "If you must know, I was thinking about when Mrs. Rockwell came to the show at my stable."

"You never really told us how you got the scholarship." Dylan leaned forward, her eyes bright with curiosity. "How did it all happen?"

Malory gritted her teeth. *I guess I asked for it. I can't really mention Diane Rockwell and then drop the subject.* She knew that if she were in the barn right now, she would have willingly poured out everything to Hardy or even Tybalt, so how come it was so much harder with her friends?

"It really wasn't that big of a deal," Malory started. "Mrs. Rockwell was passing through Cheney Falls and saw the signs for the show. She stopped off because she knew the owner of the yard — I think they trained together years ago. Anyway, she saw me riding one of the ponies there. He had acted up in an earlier class, and I got lucky and kept him on course. I guess she was impressed with that." Malory looked down and fiddled with her fork.

Diane Rockwell's exact comment had been, "You read him perfectly. You rode that pony with firmness and sensitivity. That shows a wisdom beyond your years — and as I understand it, well beyond the training you've had so far." Malory remembered those words by heart, but there was no way she was going to share that with her friends. As it turned out, she and Checkmate had placed second in the class to her friend Caleb's first, but Diane Rockwell said she wasn't as concerned with the ribbons. That very day she asked Malory to visit Chestnut Hill and try out for the scholarship that was in her name. Malory felt a tingling sensation as she remembered how psyched Caleb had been for her — even more pleased than he was with his silver cup.

"You make it sound like a one-time fluke, but you had to try out again, didn't you?" Honey prompted.

Malory nodded. "I came here and jumped Snapdragon and Shamrock in the morning. Then we had lunch in the cafeteria. I had to do dressage and take a short exam in the afternoon. I had never done dressage. Luckily Gandalf could have done it by himself, and in his sleep. After all that I had an interview with Dr. Starling." At that the girls gave a collective gasp. "My dad came with me. He said it was 'for moral support,' but I think he was more nervous than I was! At least I had the horses to keep my mind busy. All he could do was watch and worry about me making mistakes!"

She thought back to how awkwardly her dad had sipped at his tea in Dr. Starling's study. He'd managed to relax more down on the yard when Ms. Carmichael had given them a tour, although Malory hadn't been able to persuade him to take off his suit jacket, despite the sun blazing down. Suddenly she wished her dad were here right now to see how happy she was.

"Harrison campaigners at twelve o'clock," Dylan whispered.

Lynsey was heading toward them with Patience. Both girls were carrying tidy stacks of flyers. Wei Lin and Razina were by the food counter ordering their lunches, obviously feeling that they'd done their fair share to help Lynsey. Malory glanced at the dark-haired girl who was nodding enthusiastically to something Lynsey was saying to a group of Curie House seventh-graders. *No surprise that Patience is hanging on in there until the bitter end,* Malory thought.

When Lynsey approached their table, Lani held up her hand. "Don't waste your breath, sweetheart. We all know the Lynsey Harrison student council platform by now."

Dylan eyed the stack of glossy flyers. "Gee, how many rain forests were chopped down for your campaign?"

Lynsey ignored them both. "Hi, guys." She smiled around the rest of the table. "I'm just making a note of definite votes for me. I take it I can count on all of yours?"

"Isn't it supposed to be a secret ballot?" Honey asked.

Lynsey didn't miss a beat. "That doesn't mean you're not allowed to say if you'll be voting for me."

"I'm pleading the Fifth," Lani murmured to Dylan.

"Lynsey, we'd better go. You're speaking to the Granville dorm in five minutes," Patience reminded her.

Lynsey put a pile of flyers on the table. "I know you'll all make the right choice," she said before heading out of the hall.

"The right choice for the environment would be banning candidate handouts," Dylan said, looking at the flyers in the middle of the table, the glamour shot of Lynsey staring out from the front panel. Dylan gave a dramatic shudder.

"Be fair. She *is* promising to have organic soap put in every bathroom," Malory reminded her.

"Well, if money's going to get votes, then Lynsey's going to win — no contest," said Alexandra, picking up a flyer.

"I'm waiting until after the Halloween party before placing my vote," Lani decided. All of the girls running for election to the student council were helping to organize the event. Lynsey was already boasting that it was going to be the best party Chestnut Hill had ever seen.

"I just hope Lynsey's party-planning keeps her too busy to stalk Nat," said Dylan. "Did you see the way her eyes lit up the other day when she heard the Saint Kits boys would be coming?"

Malory nodded. She knew that Dylan had hated Lynsey's flirting with her cousin when he showed up at the stables earlier that term. "Just don't let her know you're worried about it," she suggested. "The last thing you want is to encourage her!" She waited uncomfortably for Dylan to ask her if she'd been in touch with Caleb about the party, but to her relief her friend turned away to argue the merits of some of the other student council candidates.

Malory's thoughts lingered on Caleb. They'd never run out of things to talk about when they hung out at the stables that summer, but suddenly she couldn't think what she was going to say if she saw him at the party that weekend.

After Saturday brunch Malory decided that she had just enough time to get down to the barn to check on Tybalt before catching the minivan into town. When she reached the far end of the aisle, Hardy stuck his head over his door.

"Here," Malory said, breaking off part of her crusty roll and holding it out to Hardy. "You can share it." Hardy gently lipped the roll off her hand and nudged her for the other bit.

"Sorry, boy." Malory laughed. "That's for your new stablemate."

She crossed the aisle to Tybalt's stall. The dark brown pony was standing at the back of the stall, watching her with his ears pricked warily. Malory noticed he had hardly touched his hay net. "Aren't you hungry?" she asked, holding out the roll. Tybalt stretched his neck toward her, but when he realized he couldn't reach the bread, he looked away.

"Come on, boy," Malory urged. Her open-toe sling-back shoes weren't exactly suitable for tramping into a stable. Tybalt looked at the roll again, but he obviously wasn't going to walk over for it. Malory shrugged and threw it into the manger. "It's there for you when you want it."

As she turned to go, she heard a rustle in the straw. Malory glanced over her shoulder and saw Tybalt dip his head into the manger and start munching the roll. It looked as if he wasn't quite as immune to tidbits as he pretended to be.

She smiled. *With a little bit of patience, he'll come through. I know he will.*

Dylan was already waiting in the van when Malory climbed in. "I thought maybe you'd changed your mind about coming," she said. "Is that because you already have everything you need for your secret costume?"

"Yeah, we've been talking, and we think you've probably plucked some leaves from the trees and are coming as Eve," Lani joked from the seat behind. "And maybe that cute boy we saw at the symposium is going to be Adam."

Malory felt her cheeks turn red. "If only I'd thought of that a few days ago," she said, trying to sound casual. She was determined not to let on that the reason she didn't have a costume was because she couldn't afford one. She regretted not saying something to Ms. Carmichael about a secondhand fleece and riding uniform. She stared out of the window as the van turned onto the main road.

Her dad had always told her that money didn't make you happy, but it sure did make things easier sometimes.

CHAPTER SEVEN

❧

When they pulled up outside the mall, Malory jumped out of the minivan and followed the others. Unlike most Saturdays when the girls scattered and headed to various destinations, today it seemed as if everyone was heading to the costume shop.

They made their way to the indoor mall, and Malory couldn't help noticing that Lynsey and Patience were lagging behind, talking in low voices. She shrugged. Whatever amazing outfits they were planning, she wouldn't get worked up about it. Lynsey was walking, talking proof that money didn't make you happy. Of all her dorm mates, Lynsey was the one who complained the most.

"This is going to be instant gratification," Dylan said as they followed Lani and Honey onto the escalator. "Find a costume today and go to the party tonight!"

Malory smiled. As long as Lynsey wasn't too close by, Dylan was all about seeing things on the bright side.

Most of the other girls were nervous about figuring out a costume in time.

Malory tipped her head back to look up at the costume store on the second level. The name of the store, Masquerade, was emblazoned in swirly black lettering against a crimson background.

They went up the escalator to the second level, and Malory paused by the store window nearest the door. Three mannequins dressed as witches sat around a smoking cauldron. "How do you think they do that?" she asked Dylan, pointing to the billowing clouds around the cauldron.

Dylan shrugged. "I don't know. It's all hocus-pocus to me. Come on!" She tugged Malory through the revolving door.

"We're going up to the top floor," Lynsey announced. "We've got a final fitting for our costumes." She glanced at her watch.

"What's your hurry?" asked Dylan. "You haven't stopped checking the time since we got in the van."

Lynsey and Patience smiled secretively. "We don't want to be late for our appointment. There's no need for us all to stick together in here." Lynsey raised her eyebrows to stall any arguments. "The rules about staying in threes can't count when we're all in the same store. There's a connected coffee shop on the main floor. We'll catch up with you in an hour."

"Yes, ma'am," Dylan muttered, pretending to salute as Lynsey and Patience walked away. She spun around to face the others. "Mal, Lani, promise me we'll all go into hiding if Ms. Harrison is ever elected president of the student council. She's way too comfortable telling others what to do!"

"It's a deal," Malory agreed.

"Who knows what they want to look at first?" asked Honey, running her fingers over a fluffy pink boa that was hanging on a mannequin.

"I don't have a clue," Alexandra admitted. "I thought I'd look in the rental department."

"Me, too," Dylan said.

"Me, three," Lani added. "Actually I just want to steal some ideas from their Lone Ranger costume. I've got leather chaps and a fringed shirt, but I want to look at the costumes here to see what I'm missing. I definitely need a mask."

Malory felt a sharp stab of envy. She'd have loved to be trying on lots of different costumes, but stayed on the fringe of the group, pretending to study a rack of glittery metallic wigs.

"Well, I want to buy a few more things for my Robin Hood outfit," Honey said.

"I'll come with you," Malory volunteered.

"When are you going to let us know what you're wearing, Mal?" Dylan prompted.

"Go!" Malory made herself laugh and flapped her hands at Dylan. "You only have fifty-eight minutes."

Dylan pulled a face as Alex and Lani linked their arms through hers and marched her away.

Malory turned to Honey. "So, what do you need to buy?"

"I already have a green suede jacket and matching shorts," Honey said as they walked over to the middle of the store. "Actually the shorts are kind of old so they're small on me. I have to get some thick green tights or I'll cause a scandal!"

Malory smiled. She wondered what would cause a bigger scandal: a demure student showing up in unbearably short shorts, or a Chestnut Hill girl not even being able to afford a costume. Maybe she'd just skip the whole party. After all, she needed all the early nights she could get if she was going to keep up with riding team practice *and* work with Tybalt.

Honey glanced at her. "Are you all right?"

"Sure, I was just thinking about how great you're all going to look."

"*We're* all going to look great," Honey corrected.

"That's what I meant," Malory said. She pulled out a quiver complete with plastic arrows, hoping to distract Honey. "Is this the kind of thing you're looking for?"

"Exactly!" Honey slung it over her shoulder and struck a pose. "How does it look?"

Malory pointed at one of the pillars in the store. "There's a mirror over there."

"I'll find the rest of the stuff before I take a peek," Honey said.

"Okay. I'll look over here." Malory walked through the wigs until she got to the hats. Almost immediately she found a green felt hat with a yellow feather sticking out of it. It would be perfect for Honey.

"I've found a bow!" Honey called.

"And I've got a hat!" Malory waved it in the air.

They took the things across to the mirror, and Malory positioned the hat at an angle on Honey's head. Her blonde hair flipped up in cute curls on each shoulder, framing her face.

"There," Malory said, spinning Honey around so she could see her reflection.

Honey beamed. "Perfect!"

"Now all you need is tights," Malory reminded her.

"Don't you need to get anything?" Honey asked, meeting her eyes in the mirror.

Malory shook her head. "I'm fine. I've got everything planned out." *I'll see you guys off like an underage fairy godmother and then will catch up on my sleep.*

Honey hesitated. "Look, Mal, I don't want to pry, but I know that putting a costume together can be expensive, especially if you're trying to make your allowance last all term."

Malory looked down at the floor. *Please don't offer to help me out with renting an outfit.* She hated the idea of her friends treating her like some charity case.

"I had to think for a long time before I came up with a costume that wouldn't force me to buy too much stuff," Honey went on. "I couldn't just walk in here and rent a complete costume."

"Really?" Malory was surprised. She'd assumed she was the only one worried about how much the Halloween party would cost.

"No way. My dad's salary from the university doesn't exactly put us in the top tax bracket," Honey told her. "They insisted that I come here, but it's a lot of money for us. I didn't even tell them about the Halloween party in case they felt bad about not giving me extra pocket money."

Malory felt a stab of empathy. "I know what you mean," she assured Honey, but she didn't offer anything more.

"Well, if you still need something for tonight, I'm willing to be your personal shopper this afternoon!"

"Thanks." Malory smiled back, but she'd already calculated the prices and knew she'd never pull anything together even close to within budget. Still, she wanted Honey to know she appreciated her thoughtfulness, so she lied. "I'll think about it, but first let's find those tights. Maybe then we can get a coffee and muffin?"

"Sounds fabulous," Honey said.

Malory headed off in search of the colored-tights aisle, hoping she'd get out of the party as easily.

☙

Malory and Honey carried their trays across to the far side of the coffee shop. They chose a high-backed booth that was covered in plastic jungle greenery. The coffee nook seemed to carry over the costume-store theme with decorations for all occasions.

As Malory took a bite out of her blueberry muffin, she saw Dylan walk in and look around. "Over here." She ducked out of the fake plants and waved.

"Hey," Dylan said, pushing a stray vine out of her hair. "Who knew someone as smart as Alex could be so indecisive? And Lani's no help. She's sending Alex in a hundred directions. We might be here a while."

Malory looked at the garment bag draped over Dylan's arm. She was also carrying an oblong package wrapped in brown paper. "Did you find a costume?"

Dylan grinned, making her eyes crinkle at the corners. "Yes! Guess what it is. No, I'll tell you. Wilma Flintstone!"

"Cool!" Honey said.

"That's hilarious," Malory agreed.

"Oh, I'm glad you like it. I'm just going to grab a

shake," Dylan said, draping the garment bag over the back of a chair.

Malory glanced at the brown package again. *It's a club!* Her lips twitched as she imagined her friend dancing around with a caveman's club.

Honey raised her eyebrows. "What's so funny?"

"I was just thinking about our dorm's obsession with weaponry. We practically have our own arsenal," Malory explained, nodding to the paper bag that held Honey's bow and arrows.

"All we need is for Alex to choose a Buffy the Vampire Slayer outfit," Honey agreed, her brown eyes sparkling. "Then we're set."

"What's up?" Dylan asked when she came back.

"We're just discussing the Adams stockpile," Honey told her, and then looked over Dylan's shoulder. "Hey, they're early. We've still got fifteen minutes to go before we arranged to meet up."

Malory turned around and saw Lynsey and Patience, both carrying garment bags over their arms. Thanks to the generous plastic leaves, they didn't seem to notice their classmates. Malory frowned when she saw them choose two separate tables. She flashed Dylan and Honey a look that asked, *Why aren't they sitting together?* Patience left her costume at her table and went over to the serving counter, but Lynsey stayed seated, flipping back her sleeve to look at her Rolex.

"There she goes checking the time again. Do you think she's meeting someone?" Honey whispered.

Dylan's eyes widened, and Malory knew exactly what she was thinking. *Please don't let it be Nat*, Malory thought. *Dylan might do some damage with her club if she sees them together on a date.*

Lynsey pulled down her sleeve. She flicked back her hair as she glanced over to the café entrance. Then she waved, her face lighting up. Malory followed her stare, crossing her fingers in the hope that she wouldn't see Dylan's red-haired cousin standing there. *Phew!* A tall, blond-haired boy wearing a Saint Kits lacrosse shirt was making his way toward Lynsey.

"Hey, check him out," Honey said.

"He's heading straight for Lynsey!" Dylan exclaimed.

They watched him pull out the chair opposite her and sit down, saying something that made Lynsey tip back her head and laugh, swooshing her blonde hair over her shoulders in a way that Malory had only seen in shampoo commercials.

"Do you think he's her boyfriend?" Dylan gulped.

"I don't think he's her brother, that's for sure," Malory replied. *He's pretty cute,* she mused to herself. This boy's breeding looked at least as impressive as Bluegrass's. *But I like dark hair better.* Malory felt her cheeks grow warm as she thought again how Caleb might be at the party that night. *But I'm not going*, she had to remind herself.

"She moves fast. Just five minutes ago she was flirting with Nat!" Dylan protested, making Malory smile at her family loyalty.

"Maybe it's their first date," Honey suggested.

"I guess we'll find out tonight," Dylan said. "I have a feeling he'll be the star of the Lynsey parade."

Malory held the last of the pins over Dylan's head, trying to secure the French twist. "If you'd stop fidgeting, I might be able to finish your hair!"

"Sorry," Dylan said. "I just can't sit still. We have only thirty minutes until our first official dance!"

"And I have only three bobby pins to go, but I'll stab you if you don't stop moving!"

Dylan was still for less than a minute before Malory said, "There. That's as close to Wilma Flintstone as I can get. No one's hair *really* does that."

At least Dylan's hair color was a perfect match for the prehistoric housewife. She applied a second coat of DuWop mascara and fluttered her eyelashes. "What do you think?"

"Hang on. You forgot your necklace," Malory said, scooping up the chunky papier-mâché stones that had come with the outfit.

Dylan and Honey had deserted their room to get ready with Lani, Malory, and Alexandra. Malory guessed

Lynsey and Patience had taken over the other room completely.

"Stick 'em up," Lani drawled, brandishing a pair of silver pistols, her eyes covered by what looked like a black satin sleeping mask with eye-shaped holes cut into it.

"Shouldn't you be saying, 'Hi-yo, Silver'?" Dylan asked. "The Lone Ranger was supposed to be a good guy, you know?"

"He was?" Lani asked dramatically. "Then how am I supposed to have any fun?"

"Well, you can hang out with us," Honey said. "We're all good guys."

Malory looked around. Honey looked great as Robin Hood, and it was a good thing they had tracked down some lime-green leggings because her hot pants were a little brief, even for the prince of thieves. Alexandra had decided to go as Pocahontas and looked really cute in a fringed suede dress. She stood by the mirror trying to make charcoal eyeliner look like war paint.

"Well, except Malory," Dylan teased. "We don't know if she is good or evil because she won't tell us what she's going to be. Aren't you cutting it close?"

Malory sat down on her bed and began to pluck at the sheet. She could tell them now or put it off longer. "Well, I'm not changing until you guys go."

"Uh-uh. You're not getting away with that." Dylan shook her head. "We're all going together."

"Yeah," Lani agreed. "How else will we make a grand entrance?" She put her hands on her hips and glared at Malory.

"Come on," Dylan said. "We won't look if you want to surprise us."

Malory looked over at Honey and bit her lip. "There is no surprise," Malory said. "I don't have a costume because I'm not going." She made herself smile. "I'm doing you a huge favor, you know. This isn't my kind of thing anyway. Just take Lani's camera and make sure you get lots of pics for me, okay?"

"You're kidding, right?" Lani said. "There's no way I'm doing that."

Malory blinked in surprise. "Okay then. I'm sure there will be someone else taking pictures."

"No, that's not the point," Lani retorted. "If you think we're going to the party and leaving you here on your own, you've lost it!" She looked at the others. "She's coming with us, right?"

"Absolutely," Dylan agreed, sitting down on the bed. "Because if you don't come, I'm not going. I'll just sit here and hit you over the head with my club all night."

"No, you won't," Malory answered defensively. This was exactly what she hadn't wanted. She didn't want anyone to feel bad for her, or for her friends to give up on their fun. She had a feeling she'd have to explain why she didn't have a costume next.

"Well, I think there's an easy way to solve this," said Alexandra. "We just need to find you a costume."

Malory looked around uncomfortably. That was the whole point. She didn't have a costume. She was fine with that. Why couldn't they be? The room went silent.

"I've got it!" Honey yelled, holding up one of Alexandra's textbooks. "Ancient civilizations!"

"There's no way she's going as a mummy," Dylan objected. "Nothing involving toilet paper."

"No, I'm thinking something much more sophisticated and not quite as dead," Honey said. She pulled back Malory's bedspread and shook her head. Then she glanced over at Lani's bed and snapped her fingers. "Lani, would you mind donating your sheet to the cause?"

"Go for it," Lani said.

Malory watched dazedly as Honey tugged off the snowy white sheet and draped it over her shoulder as if she was a mannequin. "I'm thinking ancient Egypt, with a touch of sass —"

"Cleopatra!" Alexandra exclaimed. "Oh, Malory, it's perfect for you."

Malory gave up and started laughing as her friends descended on her and guided her onto a chair.

"Okay, we need a white tank and some white shorts or a slip or something," Honey announced. Alexandra instantly provided the necessary undergarments, and Malory slipped them on.

"Give me some room; I need to unleash my genius," Lani called, waving a styling comb in one hand and a bottle of mousse in the other. She took up a handful of Malory's long wavy hair.

"Wait, let's get the dress on, and then we can deal with the hair and makeup," Dylan spoke up. The four girls began to drape and swathe the sheet over Malory's shoulder and around her waist, securing it with a gold ropelike ribbon that had been on a package Lani had received from her grandmother.

Forget about Cinderella! I've got four fairy godmothers! Malory thought as she watched her friends flitting around her and searching for Cleopatra-appropriate accessories.

"Darling, you look marvelous," Lani insisted as she rather ruthlessly teased Malory's hair to give it more lift. Feeling the tugs, Malory remembered the time her mom had braided her hair for the fourth-grade play. She had sat still for what seemed like hours as her mom wove ribbons into her hair, telling her stories about when she and Malory's dad had first met.

Honey rummaged in Dylan's makeup bag and pulled out her Kiss Me eyeliner in midnight blue. "Don't worry," Honey advised. "I'm a professional."

Malory smiled, knowing it wasn't worth protesting. Her friends were absolutely determined that she was going, and she didn't have a single excuse anymore. As

Honey began slicking blue eye shadow onto her lids, Malory closed her eyes.

She snapped out of her reverie when Dylan appeared with the straightening iron. Malory looked at the heated clamp and shuddered.

"I don't know, Dylan," she faltered. "That thing kind of scares me."

"Oh, come on," Dylan begged. "Trust me. It's for your own good."

Malory took a deep breath and crossed her fingers. "Okay, I trust you."

CHAPTER EIGHT

The deejay's heavy bass beat pounded across the lawn as the girls hurried to the gym. Colored lights flashed through the windows, and Malory fiddled with the brooch on her shoulder, hoping it would hold her makeshift costume in place.

"You look amazing," Dylan said reassuringly, as if she knew how Malory was feeling.

"Thanks to you guys," Malory replied. Her friends had totally transformed her, and she was still getting used to the effect. Dylan had straightened her curly hair with the help of nearly a whole can of mousse. Then Dylan had twisted three very thin braids on each side, so Malory looked like Elizabeth Taylor's Cleopatra. Honey's makeup artistry drew attention to Malory's eyes with a thick black outline that swept out toward her temples.

Malory glanced down at the rest of her costume. Alexandra had wrapped the sheet around her toga-style before pinning it with safety pins and Lani's brooch. Honey had loaned her some jeweled sandals while Dylan had dug out some gold-effect costume jewelry — a heavy, flat necklace and a set of bangles that felt cold and slippery on Malory's wrist. Finally Lani had used the eyeliner to draw some hieroglyphic tattoos on her upper arms. In the midst of the mousse and makeup, Malory's apprehension had given way to excitement. She fed off her friends' enthusiasm and soon found herself laughing right along.

Honey paused in front of the gym. The doors were wide open with black streamers and balloons hanging from the entrance, waving in the breeze. "Ready?"

"Now or never!" said Lani.

They walked down the corridor that led to the main hall. Each windowsill held a grinning pumpkin with a candle flickering inside.

A professor from Saint Kits was at the door talking with Ms. Marshall.

"Hi, girls. You all look great," she smiled.

Malory smiled, surprised by Ms. Marshall's all-leather ensemble. She never thought she'd see the Adams housemother for the high school students decked out in a cropped biker's jacket and black skintight leather pants.

Then, looking down, Malory remembered that she was dressed out of character herself. She'd have been a lot more comfortable in jodhpurs and her team fleece, that was for sure! Inside the hall, strobe lights flashed, lighting up a dozen figures in glaring white. Everywhere Malory looked there were weird, spooky, and kooky costumes. She stepped back to let a hooded figure carrying a scythe walk past.

Dylan, her club propped casually over her shoulder, asked, "Do you want to grab a soda?" and Malory nodded.

At the end of the hall, two long tables were covered with food and a selection of drinks.

On the other side of the hall, Malory saw someone dressed as Morticia Addams wave. She waved back. "Wei Lin's got us a table," she told the others.

As they stopped by the buffet to collect their sodas, she couldn't stop herself from scanning the gym for Caleb. She wasn't even sure he'd make an effort to say hi. Malory knew that she hadn't exactly been friendly at the symposium.

"Oh, no, check out Lynsey and Patience!" Dylan hissed, tugging at Malory's arm, almost making her spill her drink.

Malory had to admit that Lynsey looked impressive in tight black Lycra and a decidedly feline mask with shimmering whiskers. "She must have had someone sew her into that catsuit," she whispered.

When Lynsey turned to say something to Patience, Malory's attention shifted with a jolt. *Patience!* Her mouth fell open as she took in the sleek black wig, the coiled snake bracelet, and the long white dress, cinched at the waist with an elaborate jeweled-gold belt. Patience was dressed as Cleopatra.

"Get me out of here!" Malory groaned.

"Yikes." Lani took in Patience's outfit.

"You've got just as much right to be here in a Cleo costume as Patience does," Dylan pointed out.

"I know," Malory agreed. "But I'd like some time to get used to the idea — preferably before Patience finds out."

"Okay, everyone. I think Malory needs our help," Dylan announced, her face lit up in a huge grin as she motioned with her hands. Malory winced, hoping her friend wouldn't use this as an opportunity to wreak havoc.

"Adams! Fall into formation," Lani said in her best drill-sergeant impersonation, likely picked up from her air force officer father. Stifling their laughter, Alexandra, Honey, Dylan, and Lani linked arms to form a wall around Malory and then marched toward Razina and Wei Lin's table.

"Thanks, guys," Malory gasped, relieved to be able to sit down. "Patience and Lynsey are never going to believe that I didn't do this on purpose."

Razina looked up curiously. "Do what?"

"Malory's wearing the same costume as Patience," Lani announced.

"And what's more, Malory looks better." Dylan laughed.

Honey grinned. "I just think Malory put a lot more creative thought into hers." Malory had to smile in return.

"All I can say is, ouch! You've just committed the worst social offense possible," Wei Lin said, shaking her head. "I hope you've got a good lawyer."

"Oh, come on," Lani said. "This isn't as bad as what happened to Dylan. Malory wasn't trying to hurt anyone or get them into trouble. But whoever turned Dylan in had to have known Dylan would suffer."

Malory winced. It had been a while since any of them had talked about who might have told on Dylan the night she was caught jumping Morello in the moonlight. It had been part of a truth-or-dare game, and Lynsey was the one who had put Dylan up to the midnight ride. Someone had called the school officials, and Dylan had been caught. Since she had still managed to make the riding team after a two-week stable suspension, it was sometimes easy to forget that there likely was a rat in their ranks.

"Any new theories?" Lani asked.

Razina took a sip of punch. "It's no good asking me. I was convinced it was Lynsey until she swore it wasn't. Whatever other issues that girl might have, I don't think she tells lies."

Malory still wasn't one-hundred-percent sure that

it wasn't Lynsey. She knew one thing: She would bet the brooch that was holding up her outfit that it wasn't any of the girls she was sitting with. Still there were a number of people who could have done it, and it was curious that the girls who had gone to witness the dare in action — Lynsey, Patience, Wei Lin, and Lani — hadn't even received a verbal reprimand for breaking curfew.

"Maybe we'll never find out," Honey said. "It's probably best to believe that it was someone from another dorm anyway. At least that way we won't get all bitter and twisted, suspecting one another."

"You're absolutely right," Dylan replied, her face straight. "I'm much better off not knowing who it was."

Malory was relieved to hear that Dylan seemed to be letting the conversation — and the resentment — go.

"So when are we going to hit the dance floor?" Lani asked, changing the subject. "We can't hide in the corner. Sorry, but wallflower isn't really my style!"

The girls rushed the floor. The Lone Ranger and Wilma Flintstone led the way.

🐾

Nat!"

Dylan threw her arms around someone dressed in a fitted black costume with white bones painted on it. Nat turned to smile at Malory, his face heavily made up with white face paint. Malory was amazed that Dylan's cousin still looked cute under the greasy layer of makeup.

"Great costumes," he complimented everyone as he looked around the circle.

"Hey, you guys," Honey interrupted. "Lynsey's dancing with that boy!"

Malory looked where Honey was pointing and saw Lynsey laughing and dancing with the cute boy from the mall, who was dressed as Indiana Jones.

Lani turned to Nat. "Do you know who he is?"

"That's Jason Williams. He's a lacrosse goalie. And a pretty nice guy," Nat told them.

"Then what's he doing with her?" Lani asked.

As Malory watched, Lynsey reached up to adjust Jason's hat and then fix his bangs so they swept off to the side.

"Do you want to dance with us?" Dylan asked Nat. "Lani's going to show us a line dance."

"Not until I eat," Nat confessed. "Do you want to check out the buffet?"

Dylan looked around the group, and they all gave a collective shrug, then headed to the food tables.

Malory was busy investigating the chocolate bats and other desserts when she saw Lynsey and Jason approach with Patience. Her heart sank.

"Hey, guys." Lynsey had her supersweet voice on, like

they were all best buddies. "I'd like you to say hi to my boyfriend, Jason. Our moms do benefit work together."

Malory had no idea what to say. Her stomach was too busy tying itself in knots for the moment when Lynsey and Patience noticed her costume. But Patience was peering over her shoulder like she was looking for someone.

"Quit worrying. He's just fashionably late!" Lynsey told her. "Let's get some punch while we're waiting. It's from a recipe my mom got from The Four Seasons."

Is there any part of this party Lynsey hasn't had a hand in? Malory wondered.

"Sounds like they've set Patience up with one of Jason's friends," Dylan whispered, watching them move farther up the buffet table. "Hey, speaking of setting someone up . . ." She shot Malory a mischievous look before turning to Nat. "Did everyone from the eighth grade come tonight?"

"Dylan," Malory said warningly. She knew exactly what her friend was up to.

"How would I know?" Nat sounded puzzled. "Are you looking for someone in particular?"

"One of the boys you were in town with a few weeks ago," Dylan told him. "Caleb . . ." She broke off and frowned. "What's his last name?"

Malory shook her head. "Will you cut me some slack? He's just a friend, someone I hung out with during the summer. This isn't a soap opera, you know! Just because a new guy appears doesn't mean we have to take turns dating him. Look, I'm going to get some punch."

Dylan looked shocked. Malory smiled to take away any sting from her words before heading to the punch bowl. She felt annoyed at herself for letting Dylan rile her. After all, she probably thought she was doing Malory a favor by asking Nat if Caleb had come to the party.

With an audible sigh, Malory ladled some of the deep-red punch into a plastic cup.

She took a sip and then jerked the cup away from her lips. There was something in there that definitely wasn't an ice cube or a piece of fruit!

Something . . . *prickly* . . . with spiky little *legs* . . . *Disgusting!* One of the plastic spiders that was bobbing around in the silver punch bowl had made its way into her cup. She was just fishing around to get it out when a boy in a pirate costume came up to her.

"Do you want a hand?" He held up a curved black hook.

Malory laughed. "You seem to have the right tool for it." She handed over her cup. "It's like a built-in Swiss Army knife," she said with a smile.

The boy took off his eye patch and tricornered hat to see better. His dark hair fell over his forehead as he bent over her cup.

Malory stared at him in disbelief. Of course Caleb had to choose the moment when she looked like the biggest dork to come over and say hi. The last thing she wanted was to play the damsel-in-distress, save-me-from-the-plastic-spider card.

Caleb scooped up the spider on his hook and grinned at her, looking a bit self-conscious. "Maybe using my fingers would have been easier. And probably more sanitary," he speculated.

Malory remembered that look — the way he scrunched up his nose when he second-guessed himself — so very cute.

"I guess Lynsey suggested you get some punch, huh?" he asked, lifting his chin in Lynsey's direction.

Malory frowned. What was he talking about?

"You know, this whole setup feels awkward to me," Caleb went on. He tossed the spider into the punch bowl, where it landed with a little red-colored splash. "Um, anyway, your costume looks great. You know, the whole Cleopatra thing? Lynsey said you rented the last outfit they had in the store."

Malory wasn't following Caleb at all until she came upon a realization. *He thinks I'm Patience! He's the guy they set her up with! Lynsey and Jason must have persuaded him to meet her here.* She forced a smile, torn between being embarrassed at the mix-up and totally insulted that Caleb didn't recognize her.

"Lynsey doesn't know anything about my costume, actually."

It was Caleb's turn to look confused.

"Lynsey didn't tell me to get some punch," Malory said, emphasizing her words. "I'm Malory O'Neil — I rode at Cheney Falls last summer, remember?"

Caleb's blue eyes opened wide. "Oh, boy." His cheeks darkened, and he stared down at the ground and bit his lip for a moment before lifting his gaze to her eyes. "I'm sorry, Mal. It's just that your costume . . ." His voice trailed off, and he dropped his hat. As he bent down to pick it up, Malory saw Patience heading over in their direction. Adding another Cleopatra to the already sinking conversation was about the only thing that would make it more awkward.

Before Caleb straightened up, Malory bolted.

"Malory!" Dylan waved to her from where she was sitting with Lani.

Malory slumped down on one of the chairs and buried her face in her hands. "Tell me that didn't just happen."

"What did you do?" Dylan sounded bemused. "We saw Caleb head over to talk to you, and then you ditched him. Are you crazy?"

"He didn't come to talk to me. He came to talk to Patience. He thought I was her," Malory mumbled through her hands. "He didn't even remember me."

"No way," Dylan assured her. "It's just that he didn't recognize you. Have you forgotten you're in a costume?"

"Yeah, he probably just hasn't ever seen you look this good," Lani suggested.

"Thanks, Lani. I feel so much better now," Malory groaned.

"You know what she means. I doubt you ever wore a white toga to the stable," Dylan explained.

Malory looked back at the buffet table and watched Lynsey and Jason join Patience and Caleb. No matter what Dylan said, Malory had to admit that they made a good-looking foursome. Malory wasn't sure she had ever seen Patience smile so much.

She pushed back her chair. "Want to dance some more?"

Without waiting for Dylan and Lani, she went over to the dance floor, pushing through the crowd of dancers until she felt safely hidden. How could one night have so many highs and lows?

🐾

Malory, Lani, and Dylan were still dancing when the music faded and somebody tapped a microphone. Everyone around them groaned and looked to see who was interrupting the dance track.

Lynsey smiled down on everyone. Malory stared at Lynsey's black boots, which were at her eye level now that Lynsey was on the stage. The spike heels were four inches high, minimum. *How does she walk with those on?*

"Sorry to interrupt the music, guys. What can I say, except it will be worth it?" Lynsey paused and opened her made-up cat eyes wide. "As most of you know, I'm running for student council."

No way! I can't believe she's hijacked the stage to give an election speech! Malory's eyebrows shot up as she swapped glances with Dylan and Lani. Why was she the only candidate up there?

"All of the candidates were asked to help organize tonight's party, and I think you'll agree they've done a fabulous job." Lynsey began to clap.

"Someone pass a bucket. I'm about to throw up," Lani muttered.

Lynsey waited for the applause to die down and then announced, "One of my contributions tonight is a party game for the underclassmen, which I think you're all going to enjoy."

Dylan's mouth dropped open. "A *party game*. Does she think we're in kindergarten?"

"I know some of you might think party games are childish, but trust me, you're going to have fun with this one," Lynsey continued, as if she'd heard Dylan's comment. "There's a white line on the floor in the middle of the hall. I want Chestnut Hill girls on one side of the line, and Saint Kits boys on the other." She had to pause while wolf whistles and cheers echoed around the gym.

"What do we do then?" Paris Mackenzie from Curie House called out.

"Fabric bones have been hidden around each side of the room. You have to find all the bones and stick them on the black poster to make a full skeleton! First team to finish and get all the bones in the right places wins a prize." Lynsey pointed to two pieces of extra-tall poster board that had been leaned against each end of the stage.

Lynsey ran elegantly down the stairs to the floor as everyone began to clap and whistle again. She was met by a crew of stylish girls who Malory recognized as being field hockey players. They all seemed to be congratulating her on her first announcement as a student council representative, even though no one had voted yet. The music started to pulse, and people rushed toward the stage to figure out what to do.

"I sure wish I'd spent more time concentrating in anatomy," Lani said. "Where's Alex? She got an A on our last biology test."

The Chestnut Hill underclassmen quickly organized themselves into "seekers" and "assemblers." Malory was a seeker; and the moment the whistle blew, she sprinted over to one of the buffet tables and yanked up the cloth. She looked all over the polished oak floor but couldn't see anything. Just as she was about to drop the cloth, something white caught her eye. Looking up, Malory saw a cutout shape of an arm bone taped to the underside of the table. Yanking off the tape, she passed the arm to a girl she recognized from study hall, who was struggling to run across the room in her elaborate flamenco costume.

Olivia Buckley and Eleanor Dixon decided to spy on the Saint Kits skeleton and report back — at full volume — how much the boys had completed. In the end the boys finished just as the girls had found their last piece — the jawbone, which had been hidden on a mural.

Lynsey invited the Saint Kits team onto the stage and oozed with Harrison charm as she handed out the prize bags. *If she smiles much more she's going to pull a muscle,* Malory thought.

A couple of boys walked down the stairs from the stage, pulling leather dayplanners and fountain pens out of the bags.

"Wow, they must have cost her a fortune," Honey commented.

"She probably thinks it was worth every cent," said Dylan. "Now she's got every Saint Kits boy backing her. Too bad they don't vote for our student council rep."

Malory glanced around the hall to see if Caleb was anywhere nearby. She couldn't spot him, although she did see Patience dancing with Lynsey and Jason. Malory was half disappointed when she didn't see Caleb, and half relieved that he hadn't attached himself to Patience.

"Come on, Mal!" Dylan yanked her onto the dance floor. "I love this song."

Malory began to follow Dylan and Lani's enthusiastic dance moves. Things had turned out pretty well after all, considering she'd started the evening without anything to wear. She somehow had escaped being scorned for duplicating Patience's Cleopatra costume, and Caleb had talked to her. Of course, he had thought she was actually someone else at the time, but Malory decided she could deal with that.

After all, she thought with a fresh burst of optimism. *You've got to start somewhere.*

CHAPTER NINE

Malory scuffed her boot against the floor of the indoor ring. Her mouth felt as dry as the sand under her feet. The intermediate class had ended early because Ali Carmichael was bringing Tybalt up from the barn for one of them to ride. Malory wasn't sure why the trainer had decided to make Tybalt's first session at Chestnut Hill such a public spectacle.

When Malory had put Hardy back into his stall at the end of the lesson, she hadn't been able to resist peeking in on Tybalt. The gelding had been standing at the back of his stall with a saddle already on. He looked wired, his muscles all bunched up and his eyes white with worry.

"Here they come," Lani called from the entrance. She jogged over and grinned at Malory. "Have you got Velcro stitched onto your pants? I think you're going to need it!"

"Who says Malory's riding him?" Lynsey objected. She tapped her crop against the side of her boot. "It's not like she owns him."

They were distracted by Ms. Carmichael leading Tybalt in. Malory saw that he'd broken out in a sweat, and his ears flicked back as he passed under the doorway. *Hang in there, boy*, she thought. *If all goes well, you won't be looking for a new home for a very long time.*

"I imagine a number of you are interested in trying him out, so I thought we could draw a name out of a hard hat," announced Ms. Carmichael, holding Tybalt's reins in one hand and motioning with the other. "Honey, there's a hat with names over by the door. Could you draw one out, please?"

"He looks like he's got good breeding," Lynsey said, running her eyes over the dark mahogany gelding.

"And we all know that's what counts," Dylan said sarcastically.

Privately Malory agreed that Tybalt looked impressive. He held his head high, and there was a noticeable kink in his tail.

"I'd say he has thoroughbred blood, with a touch of Arab," Lynsey pronounced, looking at Tybalt's dished face. "He seems pretty sure of himself. He's going to need someone who understands how to ride a high-strung horse."

Lani rolled her eyes. "Thank goodness you're here,

Lynsey. The rest of us wouldn't have a clue what to do."
Lynsey rolled her eyes in return.

Honey went over to get the hat. *Please let me be the one
to ride him,* Malory thought, watching Honey rummage
in the pile of folded papers. She held her breath as Honey
chose one and opened it.

"Lynsey," she read.

Malory felt a razor-sharp stab of disappointment. Of
all people.

Dylan squeezed her arm sympathetically. "Sorry."

The fact that Lynsey's name had been drawn first made
it a hundred times worse. Malory bit her lip, wishing she
didn't feel like it was so unfair. Lynsey was an excellent
rider — she'd probably had more private lessons than
the rest of the class put together. And maybe there was
some truth in her comment about Tybalt needing a rider
who was used to handling a high-strung pony.

Lynsey walked over to Ms. Carmichael, who was
waiting to give her a leg up. "I can manage, thanks," she
said, placing her foot into the stirrup and swinging herself into the saddle.

Malory hugged herself as she watched Tybalt walk
forward with his ears flat back. Lynsey shortened her
reins and pushed him into a trot. Tybalt tucked his nose
in so that it looked like Lynsey had him under control;
his neck was so stiff that Malory was certain he wasn't at

all happy. Her fingernails bit into her palms. *Why won't she just loosen her reins?*

"Give him some more rein, Lynsey," Ms. Carmichael called.

Lynsey pushed her hands forward a little, but Malory thought her priority was still keeping Tybalt under control, rather than letting him find his own pace.

Lynsey stopped circling at the far end of the ring and rode down the center line. She changed from a posting to a sitting trot, looking straight ahead. As Tybalt passed the center of the ring, he suddenly veered toward the gate. Lynsey let out a hiss of frustration, closing her outside leg on him and pulling the inside rein. Tybalt pulled against her until Lynsey let go of the reins with one hand and tapped him with a crop behind her outside leg.

Malory saw a wild look flash in Tybalt's eyes and knew that he was about to lose it.

Tybalt jerked his head down, yanking Lynsey forward. Before she had time to regain her balance, Tybalt gave a huge buck. Lynsey fell forward onto his neck, and the gelding twisted sideways, shaking her off. She landed with a thud, and the ring went silent. At once, everyone raced over to help her as Tybalt bolted down to the far end of the arena.

Oh, Tybalt. Malory's heart flipped when she saw him skid to a halt beside the gate. He was trembling all over.

Although she wanted to run over to comfort him, she knew that would probably unravel him even more. Besides, she knew she needed to check on Lynsey, like the rest of the girls.

Lynsey was stunned at first, but she promptly stood up. In response to everyone's murmurs of "Are you okay?" she simply said, "I'm fine." When Malory arrived, Lynsey was busy brushing the sand off her jodhpurs. "That is a dangerous animal!" she said furiously. "There's no way he should be at Chestnut Hill."

"Calm down, Lynsey," Ms. Carmichael said. "Malory, will you please catch Tybalt? I'll want to take a look at him."

Lynsey's fingers trembled as she yanked off her hat and shook back her hair. "I can tell you now, there's no way Liz Mitchell would have bought a horse like that."

Even though Malory was walking away, Lynsey's voice was still loud and clear.

"He's unridable. That's exactly why I brought my own pony to this school. We certainly won't beat Allbrights on horses like this." She snatched up her crop and stormed out of the arena.

Malory couldn't believe Lynsey had the nerve to speak to a faculty member like that.

"Malory, when you're ready would you please take Tybalt to his stall? Everyone else, class dismissed. I need to have a talk with Miss Harrison," Ms. Carmichael said calmly as she followed Lynsey toward the door.

Malory nodded and waited for the Director of Riding to leave the arena before turning toward Tybalt again.

Dylan broke the silence. "I hope she takes that crop of Lynsey's and shows her a more creative way of using it."

Dylan had put into words what Malory had felt guilty for thinking. Right now, though, she had something else to worry about. She made herself walk slowly toward the gelding.

He laid back his ears, and Malory knew he was ready to run again. Trying to think of the most nonconfrontational way to get close to him, she turned around. She took one step backward and paused. Then she took another. This would be the best way of reaching him without threatening him. When she sensed she was within an arm's distance, she reached for the reins before turning around. Tybalt sighed like all the fight had gone out of him.

"Good boy," Malory murmured, straightening his mane. "You're going to be okay. I promise."

She then let out her own sigh. She knew Lynsey had overstepped the line, no doubt about it. But Tybalt was in just as much trouble as Lynsey was. And once she'd dealt with Lynsey, Ms. Carmichael would be back to deal with him.

❧

Malory buckled a cooling sheet on Tybalt and put a light blanket on top of that. Even though she had rubbed him down and sponged him, the gelding kept breaking out in a damp sweat.

He stood in his stall, staring at the wall as if he was locked in his own world. Malory would almost have preferred him to be agitated and angry. She hated the dull look in his eyes and the way he was hanging his head.

She was beginning to think there was more to Tybalt's behavior than being moved from one new place to the next. He wasn't just unsettled — he was genuinely scared. And Malory had the feeling that he was sensitive enough to know he had done something wrong. She ran her hand down his neck before holding out an alfalfa cube. He lipped it off her hand; but instead of chewing it, he dropped it onto the floor.

Dylan looked over the door. "How's he doing?"

"Not great. He's worse than before," Malory admitted.

"Maybe he'll be better the next time," Dylan suggested. "Maybe he . . . just needed to work through some stuff."

Malory smiled at Dylan, appreciating her friend's horse-shrink attempts. "I sure hope so."

"Me, too." Dylan suddenly turned serious. "Because if he doesn't settle in soon, Aunt Ali will have to send him back. She can't have a horse on the yard that isn't earning its keep, no matter how gorgeous he is."

Malory leaned against Tybalt. That was the last thing she wanted to hear, not just for her sake, but for Tybalt's as well. His similarity to Zanzibar, while it still took her breath away, no longer seemed important. Now she felt a true connection to the pony right in front of her. *If we give up on Tybalt and send him back, who knows what will happen to him?*

Malory had convinced herself that Chestnut Hill was the pony's last hope.

❦

Malory was in the gym locker room. Her Spanish class was on the other side of campus, and she was going to have to run all the way if she didn't want to be late. She scooped her shoe from the locker and sat down on the bench to buckle it. A door banged in the hallway, and she heard Lynsey's voice outside, speaking to their gym teacher.

"It won't be a problem, Ms. Feist. I'll just ask permission from Ms. Carmichael to skip my riding lesson this Friday. I'm sure she'll understand."

"I'll need written permission before I pencil you in for the hockey-team tryouts," Ms. Feist warned. "I'll need the note by Thursday at the latest."

Malory sat up in surprise. *What is Lynsey up to? She can't try out for the hockey team — she's already on the junior jumping team. Isn't there a school rule that you can't be on more than one competition team per season?*

She grabbed her bag and hurried out of the locker room. Malory pushed open the double doors and saw Lynsey halfway down the corridor.

"Lynsey, wait up!" Malory ran down the corridor after her.

Lynsey turned around.

"You're not really trying out for the field hockey team, are you?" Malory gasped when she reached the end of the hall.

Lynsey raised one eyebrow. "I don't remember telling you my personal plans." She stressed the word *personal*.

"But we're in the middle of practicing for our next show," Malory protested, even though she knew she shouldn't push the point. "It's only two weeks away!"

"I'm well aware of that," Lynsey said icily as she pushed through the doorway. "I guarantee Blue and I will be ready, which is more than I can say about some team members." She paused to let her insult sink in and then said, "Besides, I can try out for as many teams as I want. My sisters did. And with their success, there's not a sports team here that wouldn't want me to try out." She looked Malory up and down. "I don't see why I should have to rationalize myself to you."

Before Malory could respond, Lynsey turned away and took the path heading back to Adams House. Malory got the message loud and clear: Lynsey didn't think it was any of her business.

Malory shook her head. Lynsey had also been elected as a student council junior representative — Dr. Starling had announced the results in the assembly yesterday. She wondered exactly how Lynsey thought she would be able to juggle everything. *If she's not careful*, Malory realized as she rushed to Spanish class, *Lynsey Harrison is going to crack.*

🐾

Malory curled up on one of the sofas in the lounge with a magazine article on Amy Fleming's work. She had read it a dozen times already but was hoping she might be able to find some extra hints. If ever there was a horse needing a special, alternative approach, Tybalt was it.

Dylan and Lani were taking on Honey and Alex in a Ping-Pong match on the other side of the room, and judging from the loud string of complaints, Honey and Alex were in the lead. Malory smiled at her friends' obvious enthusiasm, but she noticed Lynsey and Patience roll their eyes as they entered the sitting room.

The two girls curled up on the sofa opposite Malory and smiled at each other. Neither of them looked at Malory — which suited Malory just fine. "So what are you going to wear on Saturday?" Lynsey asked. "My advice is to wear something dressy on top, but keep it casual with jeans. You don't want to overwhelm Caleb on the first date."

Malory caught her breath. Patience and Caleb were going on a *date*? She stared at the page of her magazine, but it blurred. She had been so interested in finding out if Amy Fleming's methods would work on Tybalt, but now she was completely distracted.

Patience scooped up her dark hair. "That sounds good, and then maybe I could wear my hair up," she said earnestly.

"Yes, with those gorgeous amber earrings your dad sent you." Lynsey laughed. "Caleb will forget all about the movie."

Malory tried to ignore the hurt that was rising inside her. She wouldn't have thought Patience was Caleb's type in a million years, but he'd obviously liked her enough after the party to ask her out. *What are the chances that he'd be interested in a scholarship girl?* asked a voice in her head. But one of the reasons Malory had liked Caleb last summer was that he hadn't acted like the kind of guy who'd let that kind of thing bother him. He had seemed far more interested in horses and riding than dating.

The other two girls continued to discuss clothing combinations for their upcoming double date. Malory knew they hadn't been aware of her crush on Caleb, so she had no reason to think they were trying to make her jealous. Malory felt a stab of relief that she hadn't even fully admitted her crush to Dylan; at least that would make it easier to convince herself that it had never even existed.

🐿

Malory slowed Hardy as they approached the upright. If he didn't knock it down, they would have a clear round! In the last three strides before the fence, she gave him plenty of encouragement with her seat and legs, and felt like cheering out loud as he sailed over the fence.

"Well done, Malory!" Ms. Carmichael called.

Malory cantered Hardy in a circle before bringing him back to the group.

"That's it for this class. Junior team, I expect you to be practicing extra hard now that the show is less than two weeks away. We need everyone here, for every session." Ms. Carmichael didn't mention Lynsey's name, but it was obvious she wasn't happy that a team member was missing today's practice.

"Did you hear that Eleanor Dixon got mad at Lynsey when she found out about the hockey tryouts?" Dylan asked as they rode out of the arena.

Malory nodded. "Lynsey pointed out that she gets straight A's in all her classes, so she can afford to take on more activities than the rest of us mere mortals."

"Eleanor didn't really go for that," Dylan said with a

shake of her head. "I just hope Lynsey knows what she's doing."

They dismounted before leading the horses into the barn. As she ran up Hardy's stirrups, Malory noticed Kelly leading Tybalt in from the field. The dark brown gelding pricked his ears when he saw Malory.

Kelly halted him while she waited for the intermediate class to take their ponies into the barn, but Malory led Hardy over to say hi. She'd tried to spend at least half an hour every day with Tybalt since he'd arrived. He'd even been waiting for her — or for the sliced carrot he knew she'd bring — with his head over the door last night. For the first time, Malory had let herself think he might be settling into his new home and growing accustomed to his new friends.

"He looks like he's in a good mood," she said to Kelly as she reached out to stroke Tybalt's nose.

Kelly nodded. "But he still isn't used to being turned out with the others. He's more interested in hanging over the fence to hang out with the cows in the next field!"

Suddenly Tybalt laid back his ears and let out a high-pitched squeal. Before either girl could react, he swung his hindquarters around and kicked at Hardy.

Hardy skidded backward, pulling Malory with him.

"Whoa, boy!" she called, trying to calm him. Then she looked down in dismay. A stream of blood ran down Hardy's leg.

"That's all we need," Kelly groaned. "Keep him here while I put Tybalt in his stall and get Ms. Carmichael. I don't think we should move Hardy until she's seen him."

Malory watched in dismay as Kelly led Tybalt away. His movements were stiff and he swished his tail restlessly as he passed another pony. He obviously wasn't improving at all if he still had issues with the other horses. And he'd just lashed out at Malory's mount for the junior jumping team. Malory crossed her fingers hopefully. If Hardy was lame, she would be out of the competition.

CHAPTER TEN

Malory raced down to the stables first thing the next morning. Since it was Saturday, she didn't have to worry about cutting short her visit for the start of morning classes.

Hardy was lying in a deep bed of straw. He nickered softly when he saw Malory but didn't get up.

"Poor boy," she whispered, looking at his bandaged hind leg. Ms. Carmichael had cleaned and dressed the wound the night before and had arranged for the vet to come by this morning. Malory hoped she was in time to hear what the veterinarian had to say about the injury. Hardy had to get better before the Saint Kits show. He just had to!

She pulled back the bolt on the door and stepped carefully across the straw. Hardy raised his head to watch her. When Malory sat down alongside him and began to stroke his neck, he dropped his head back down with a sigh.

Malory began to move her fingers in slow circles on

his neck. She hummed quietly, watching Hardy's ears flicker. *I'm sorry I was stupid. It's my fault you got hurt,* she thought for the hundredth time. *I should have known Tybalt would have felt defensive.*

Hardy lifted his head again at the sound of voices coming from the aisle. With a low moan he scrambled to his feet, keeping his weight off his bad leg.

"Hello, Malory. How long have you been here?" Ms. Carmichael smiled over the door at her.

Malory stood up, brushing bits of straw off her clothes. "Not long. I wanted to see how Hardy was." She glanced at the auburn-haired woman behind Ms. Carmichael. She was wearing a battered yard coat and carrying a heavy brown leather case.

"This is Dr. Olton," said Ms. Carmichael, opening the door. "She's come to take a look at Hardy's leg."

"I'll check on Tybalt," Malory offered, wanting to give the veterinarian room to examine Hardy. She crossed the aisle and let herself into Tybalt's stall.

The dark brown gelding looked around from his hay net. Malory was relieved to see that he continued to munch his hay as she walked over to him. A week ago he would have swung away from her and stopped eating altogether. There was no doubt he was feeling more comfortable in his new home, but he still had a lot of issues to work through in terms of being ridden and being around other horses.

Malory straightened his blanket. "Why did you have to kick Hardy?" she murmured. "He wasn't bothering you."

His water bucket was empty so she took it to the tap at the end of the barn. After she brought it back, she decided to get a brush and groom him. Anything to keep busy! She was dreading hearing Dr. Olton's verdict on Hardy — he had looked so sorry for himself that it was hard to imagine he would be healthy by the competition. But a tiny part of Malory clung to the hope that Tybalt had just given him a light bruise, and he'd be fine after a few days' rest.

She ran a body brush over Tybalt's chocolate-brown coat, sweeping it over his muscled quarters and down his long legs.

"How is he?" Ms. Carmichael asked, resting her arms on the door.

"He seems fine." Malory straightened up. "What about Hardy?"

Ms. Carmichael paused. "It's not good news, I'm afraid. Dr. Olton thinks he's cracked a bone in his back leg. It will heal, but he needs complete rest for at least two months."

Malory's mouth felt dry. "Is he in a lot of pain?"

"Well, it's hard to say. It's obvious that he's pretty uncomfortable, but it shouldn't be anything too extreme. The vet prescribed anti-inflammatory drugs, and we'll have to hose his leg every day for the next week to bring the swelling down."

"I feel like an idiot for taking Hardy up to Tybalt." Malory wanted Ms. Carmichael to know that it wasn't Tybalt's fault, that they shouldn't punish him for hurting Hardy.

Ms. Carmichael shrugged. "You didn't know Tybalt would react like that. I wouldn't have suspected it, either. But if he's going to be a Chestnut Hill horse, he's going to have to learn to get along with other horses."

Malory glanced up with her heart thudding hopefully. "You mean you aren't going to send him back?"

"Well, he's been more of a challenge than I'd have liked," Ms. Carmichael admitted. "But I promised to give him a month." She paused. "Try not to get too hopeful, though, Malory. It doesn't mean Tybalt's a bad horse if he doesn't fit in at Chestnut Hill. We need a pretty special kind of pony around here."

But Tybalt is special! Malory thought, yet she knew her instinct wasn't enough proof. It would be up to her to convince Ms. Carmichael that he should stay. She picked up Tybalt's empty food bucket and headed for the door.

Ms. Carmichael held it open for her. "I'm sure you realize that you're not going to be able to ride Hardy for the show."

Malory stopped dead. She'd been so upset to hear the vet's diagnosis that she hadn't given any thought to the competition, even though it had seemed so important before.

"I'd like to pair you up with Foxy Lady," Ms. Carmichael went on. "She went well for you when you tried her out. What do you think?"

"Yes, sure," Malory answered automatically. Foxy Lady had been a great ride, but Malory thought she probably would have jumped like that for anyone. Malory preferred horses that weren't such an easy study — horses that responded best to a rider with whom they had built an understanding. For Malory, those were the most rewarding.

She looked at Tybalt. His coat gleamed, and she could see the muscles flex in his neck as he pulled at his hay net. He looked to be in good shape even though he hadn't been worked much lately. A crazy idea began to form in Malory's head. *He's a fantastic mover, and not even Lynsey could find fault with his breeding. Maybe he can jump, too?*

"What about Tybalt?" she blurted out. "We could give him a second chance and, if he goes okay, I could take him."

Ms. Carmichael pushed a strand of dark hair off her forehead and looked thoughtful. "I tell you what," she said. "You can try him out in the outdoor ring this afternoon, and we'll see how he goes for you, okay?"

Malory grinned. "It's a deal!"

"Don't get your hopes up," Ms. Carmichael warned. "I'd love for Tybalt to settle in and find his stride here, but it's not going to happen overnight. Maybe not even in the next couple of weeks." She slid the bolt home on Tybalt's stall door. "He's got a lot to prove. I'll see you down in the outdoor arena at two o'clock."

Malory waited for the riding instructor to get to the end of the aisle before she let out a whoop. *I know we'll show her*, she thought, looking at Tybalt. She was already picturing him soaring over fences with inches to spare, to the sound of rapturous applause from the packed bleachers. *Today's the first test, and then we'll go from there.*

❧

Tybalt didn't seem quite as sure of Malory's plan. By the time she led him down to the outdoor arena, his tail was raised, and dark patches of sweat darkened his flanks. Sarah was pushing a wheelbarrow across the yard, and Tybalt spooked as it squeaked by. Malory reached up her hand to soothe him, realizing with dismay that he was even more tense than when Lynsey had ridden him.

Ms. Carmichael was waiting for her, holding the gate wide open so Malory could lead him straight in.

Tybalt shifted uneasily when she mounted. "Easy," she murmured. She squeezed with her legs, and Tybalt moved forward at a short, choppy walk.

"Trot when you reach the corner," Ms. Carmichael called.

Malory shortened her reins and squeezed Tybalt again, but instead of going forward, he swung his quarters off the rail. When she urged him to straighten with her inside leg, he let out a squeal of protest.

I've got to give Lynsey credit, Malory thought. *I might not even get him to trot.* She was hit with the grim reality of just how difficult Tybalt was to ride. Sitting deeply, she asked him to move forward, but the brown gelding resisted. Yanking the reins out of Malory's hands, he thrust his head down and bucked. Malory leaned back in the saddle, fighting to keep her balance.

"I think you'd better get off!" Ms. Carmichael told her.

Malory dropped her stirrups and swung off Tybalt, keeping ahold of his reins. Hot tears burned behind her eyes, and she shook her head fiercely. Right now she had to focus on calming Tybalt.

"Steady, boy," she soothed, reaching out her hand.

The brown gelding ran a full circle around her before she managed to get him to halt.

"Well, I guess that settles it," Ms. Carmichael said, coming over. "You'll have to practice on Foxy Lady for the show." She ran her hand down Tybalt's damp neck. "He's a lovely mover, but I've come across horses like this before. He might need more than we can give him." She sighed. "I'm sorry, Malory. I know you have a lot of hopes for him, but I can't risk letting students ride him."

In her heart of hearts, Malory knew Tybalt had blown

his last chance. If he couldn't trot around the ring, there was no way he'd find a place at Chestnut Hill.

He just doesn't fit the mold. Just like me, she figured ruefully. *No wonder I felt such a connection with him.* She wondered what would happen if, someday, someone gave up on her, too.

🖦

After she rubbed Tybalt down, Malory wandered toward the lake. She looked out over the water, squinting as the sun glinted off the surface.

I've made a complete mess of things. It would have been better if I had never persuaded Ms. Carmichael to bring Tybalt here. Better for him — and better for me.

She sat down on the grassy bank and lay back with her head on her arms. She closed her eyes, feeling the sun's rays soak through her clothes.

"I hear the practice session didn't go so well."

Malory opened one eye to see Dylan standing over her.

"It was a total disaster," she admitted as her friend sat down beside her. "How did you know where to find me?"

"Madison Ashcroft came into the student center and said she'd seen you heading this way, looking pretty upset." Dylan propped herself up on one arm. "What happened?"

"Tybalt did exactly the same thing to me that he did to

Lynsey," Malory told her. "Actually that's a lie. I couldn't even get him to trot."

Dylan tipped her head to one side. "So I guess this means you're ready to give up on him?"

Malory plucked a blade of grass and began tearing it into small pieces. "I don't *want* to give up," she said stubbornly. "But he doesn't want to connect with anyone — not even other horses, which is totally weird. It's like he's got this brick wall built up around him, and I don't know how to break it down."

"You need someone who has all the right demolition tools," Dylan agreed. "Someone who won't be fazed by his attitude."

"Exactly. I wish I could find someone who doesn't care if he's right for Chestnut Hill. Someone who will just try to reach him as a horse first, and then we can see about all the other stuff." Malory sighed. What were the chances of finding someone like that?

Suddenly she stared at her friend, her mind going into overdrive.

"Amy Fleming!" Both girls spoke together.

Malory jumped up. "Do you really think she'd help? I've been reading every article about Heartland that I could find, but I never thought of actually asking her!"

"Sending her an e-mail isn't going to hurt any," Dylan said. "Come on, let's go ask Aunt Ali for her address."

As they ran around the edge of the lake, Malory suddenly

felt more positive than she had in days. If Amy Fleming agreed to look at Tybalt, Malory knew she'd have given Tybalt every chance to prove himself. He didn't *have* to be a Chestnut Hill horse, but she hoped he could be happy.

☞

"Come in," Ms. Carmichael's voice called in reply to Malory's knock.

Malory crossed her fingers and shot an apprehensive smile at Dylan before stepping into the office.

The wall behind Ms. Carmichael's desk was lined with shelves holding books and files, but Malory's gaze rested on the other walls that were covered with pictures of fabulous horses. Beneath the window was a long glass cabinet filled with trophies and rosettes, most of them blue.

"Do you have Amy Fleming's e-mail address?" Dylan blurted out before Malory had a chance to speak.

Ms. Carmichael laced her fingers together. "I think I do. I'm sure she was copied on the e-mails we sent about the symposium." She raised an eyebrow questioningly.

"We figured she might be able to help Tybalt," Malory explained. "She said that she'd treated lots of horses with behavioral problems —"

Ms. Carmichael held up her hand. "I appreciate your idea, girls, but Amy Fleming is a very busy person. When she's not studying at Virginia Tech, she works full-time at Heartland."

"Well, even if she couldn't come see him, maybe she could give us some advice," Malory persisted. There was no way she was giving up that quickly.

"If you e-mailed her, she might want to help," Dylan added. "This is her specialty, isn't it?"

Malory glanced at her friend. Dylan was using such a casual tone that Malory knew she was not asking the question to Ms. Carmichael, the riding instructor, but to Ali Carmichael, her aunt. The room was silent for a moment, and Malory was afraid to breathe. She hoped Dylan hadn't stepped over the line.

"Okay, you've persuaded me." Ms. Carmichael smiled. "I'll e-mail her today."

Malory let out a sigh of relief. "That would be great, thanks."

"I'll let you know what she says as soon as I get her answer," Ms. Carmichael promised.

🐃

Malory pushed open the doors to the Liberal Arts building and pounded down the corridor. She knew she wasn't supposed to run but right now she didn't care. *Amy Fleming was going to visit Tybalt!*

The rest of the students were already inside the English classroom. Malory put her head around the door, realizing that the teacher had already started her lesson.

"'And fill me from the crown to the toe top-full of direst cruelty!'" Ms. Griffiths was reading aloud from *Macbeth*.

"Sorry I'm late. Ms. Carmichael needed to speak with me," Malory apologized.

"It's all right just this once. Take your seat and turn to Act One, Scene Five," Ms. Griffiths told her.

Malory walked up the aisle and caught Dylan's questioning glance. Malory grinned in reply.

"Way to go!" Dylan's congratulatory whisper sounded more like a loudspeaker announcement.

The rest of the class broke into giggles.

"Sorry," Dylan muttered.

"Dylan Walsh, since you seem to be bursting with enthusiasm today, I think it would be a great idea for you to come to the front of the class and read the part of Lady Macbeth." Ms. Griffiths' finger tapped against the leather binding of her Shakespeare collection.

"Yes, Ms. Griffiths." Dylan pushed her chair back, looking more than happy with her penalty. Malory knew she loved drama.

She tried to follow as Dylan read Lady Macbeth's spine-chilling speech, but her thoughts kept drifting to what would happen when Amy Fleming visited the next day. Ms. Carmichael had told her that Amy had e-mailed to say she had a Wednesday afternoon off every week, and she'd come out to see Tybalt then. *Maybe she'll join up with him*. Malory remembered the video that Amy had shown of her working with her own horse, Spindleberry. She half closed her eyes and imagined herself standing in the center of the ring with Tybalt cantering around her, his dark mane blowing in the breeze.

Her eyes shot open when something small and hard smacked the side of her head. A paper pellet bounced onto the desk in front of her.

"Earth to Malory," Lani whispered.

Malory blinked. She looked up and noticed that Ms. Griffiths wasn't at the front of the class anymore.

"She went to get a DVD of *Macbeth* for us to watch," Honey explained. She left her chair and came to perch on Malory's desk. "So now you can tell us what's going on."

Malory beamed up at them. "Amy Fleming's coming tomorrow afternoon!"

"Ms. Carmichael's bringing in a horse shrink?" Lani teased.

"That horse needs more than a shrink." Lynsey turned in her chair. "I've told Ms. Carmichael that I don't want Bluegrass anywhere near him. She might be happy risking the school horses and her students, but Bluegrass is way too valuable to take any chances with."

"Nice to see you thinking of others, as usual," Dylan said sarcastically.

"Well, someone's got to think of Blue, and he is my horse, after all," Lynsey said, missing the point of Dylan's comment. She glanced meaningfully at Patience. "I would have thought that Ms. Carmichael would have been able to sort out any problem horses herself. I can't imagine that Liz Mitchell would have stooped to bringing in unqualified help if she were still here. Then again, she never would have bought such an unpredictable animal."

Patience nodded loyally. "I bet Allbrights has the best school horses."

Uh-oh. Malory glanced over to see Dylan's reaction to Lynsey and Patience's side-discussion.

Dylan was wearing her sweetest smile — a sure sign trouble was brewing. She sauntered over to Lynsey's desk and peered down at Lynsey's notebook.

"You know your work is starting to look distinctly sloppy, Harrison," she said, lifting her finger to her chin in a pronounced way. "I'd say you'd be lucky to get a B. Maybe instead of trying to involve yourself in every activity — and every conversation — that is going on in the school, you should concentrate a little more on *your own business*."

"Ms. Griffiths is coming!" Razina whispered loudly from her desk by the door.

While the girls scrambled back to their chairs, Malory noticed that Lynsey's cheeks had drained of color. She guessed that Dylan had hit a raw nerve. *Maybe Lynsey's under more pressure than we realize*, she thought, watching

Lynsey drop her head and stare at the page in front of her. *It can't be easy having to follow in the steps of two ultrasuccessful sisters.*

Malory shook her head, knowing that few people had sympathy to spare for their social-climbing classmate. Lynsey was highly selective about which girls she considered friends, and she seemed to look down on almost everyone else. But, when it came to personal expectations, Malory was starting to see that Lynsey could be her own worst enemy, which was saying a lot with Dylan Walsh around!

CHAPTER ELEVEN

Malory stared at the clock for the hundredth time. She glanced back at the periodic table that Ms. Marshall had handed out for study period, but it may as well have been written in ancient Greek for all the sense it was making right now. It was the next afternoon. Amy Fleming had promised to arrive between four and five. *Maybe she's down at the stables with Tybalt now.* Malory's mouth was dry. *What if she's already told Ms. Carmichael she can't help him?*

Ms. Hutson waited right up until the bell rang before looking up from her sketch pad. "You can go now."

Malory stuffed her books into her bag, dropping her pen on the floor.

"Relax. She might not even be there yet." Dylan bent down to pick up the pen.

Malory zipped up her bag. "Are you coming?"

"I'm going to grab a snack, and then I'll be down. Do you want me to get you anything?"

Malory shook her head.

"I'll see you in five minutes or so," Dylan promised.

But Malory was already heading for the door. She didn't want to miss a single moment of Amy Fleming's visit — or a word of her advice!

🐎

Amy Fleming and Ms. Carmichael were talking quietly outside Tybalt's door. They looked around at the sound of Malory's footsteps.

"Hi, Malory." Ms. Carmichael smiled. "This is Amy Fleming."

"Hi, Ms. Fleming. Thanks so much for coming. I really enjoyed what you said about your work at Heartland," Malory enthused. She broke off, wondering if she sounded a bit dorky.

"Thank you." The vet student gave a short laugh. Her gray eyes were warm. "Please call me Amy. I really enjoyed giving my talk. It's nice to know you appreciated it."

"I've just introduced Amy to Tybalt," Ms. Carmichael told Malory.

"What did you think of him?" Malory asked eagerly.

"He's lovely," Amy said. "But he's kind of nervous, isn't he?"

"You can say that again," said Malory. Amy was so friendly and down-to-earth that it was hard to remember she'd never met her before. It felt as if Malory had known her for ages. "He seems so unhappy, which is what worries me the most! He doesn't like being ridden, or having people around him. He doesn't even like the other horses. Kelly told me he spends most of his time watching the cows in the other field when he's turned out."

"I heard about how he acted when you tried riding him, too," Amy said. "I'd like to find out about his background. Sometimes when troubled horses come to Heartland, finding out about their past really helps. Ms. Carmichael gave me the number of the stable he came from, so I'll call later on. But whatever went on in the past, Tybalt looks as if he has a basically sweet nature." She pulled back the bolt on the door and stepped in. "He's got large eyes that aren't too close together, and if you look on the middle of his forehead you can see his hair grows in a swirl. That usually means a trustworthy temperament."

Malory watched Tybalt swing his head around to sniff at Amy. He didn't retreat to the back of his stall as usual, but pricked his ears forward and blew through his nose. *She really does understand horses on a whole different level,* Malory thought.

"I've brought a few natural remedies that might help Tybalt relax," Amy said, reaching into her pocket. She pulled out a plastic bag that held three bottles. "I've mixed together some grapefruit seed extract, lavender, marjoram, vetiver, and orange in this. It's an aromatherapy treatment to spray in his stall."

Malory went over to take a closer look. She pointed at a small brown bottle with a glass dropper. "Is that one of the Bach Flower Remedies you mentioned in your talk?"

Amy nodded. "Good memory. You can put the liquid in Tybalt's water or let him lick a few drops off your hand." She unscrewed the third bottle and a strong aroma filled the stall. "We'll use this to calm him down before we take him down to the arena."

"Lavender, right? I've heard it's good for nervous horses," Ms. Carmichael said, joining them.

"It's unbeatable," Amy agreed. "Horses can't ingest it, though — that means they can't drink it like they do the Bach Flower Remedies," she added, seeing Malory look confused. "Instead, we can massage a little into Tybalt's coat using T-touch."

"I remember that from the symposium," Malory said. "Are you going to do it now?"

Amy smiled. "It's a great way of calming horses. It helps release tension that they're holding in their muscles and increases body awareness, so they are less likely to respond with fear." She wrinkled her forehead and made a face like she was flinching. "What a bore!" she exclaimed. "I sound like I'm giving a lecture!"

"No, no. It's very interesting," Ms. Carmichael said. She took a deep breath as Amy tipped a few drops into the palm of her hand. "I wish I could get this treatment at the end of a long day," she said.

Amy laughed. "You could always go to a spa, but I'm sure Tybalt wouldn't mind sharing. Now we need to massage it into his coat in slow circles. I'll show you first, and then Malory can take over. Sound okay to you, Ali?" Ms. Carmichael nodded, so Malory moved closer to watch Amy's fingers move in small circles down Tybalt's neck.

"I've been trying to do this myself," Malory admitted. "I'm not sure I'm any good, though."

"Let me see," Amy said encouragingly. She put some drops of oil onto Malory's hand and stood back. "Think about making tiny circles with your fingertips, following the lie of his coat."

Feeling a little self-conscious, Malory began to rub the oil into Tybalt's neck. She focused so hard that after a while she forgot about Amy and Ms. Carmichael watching her. Gradually she could feel Tybalt's muscles soften under her fingers.

"That's great," Amy murmured behind Malory. "He's definitely responding to you."

Tybalt lowered his head and sighed. His eyes were half closed, and his ears flopped forward. Malory felt a thrill of amazement that T-touch actually worked.

"I think he's ready to be taken out to the ring now," Amy said. "I'd like to try to joining up with him so I can help him begin to regain his trust in people."

Malory reached up to push Tybalt's long dark forelock

away from his eyes. Amy's optimism was infectious. Once again she pictured Tybalt flying over a course of jumps, racing against the clock to take the blue ribbon for the junior jumping team. Then she remembered how disastrously her schooling session had gone, and her heart sank. She had all kinds of faith in Tybalt, but he hadn't shown an ounce of it in her.

🐎

Wait up!" Dylan was pelting down the track that led to the outdoor arena. Malory held the gate for her before shutting it. They climbed the fence and sat on the top rail.

"What's happening?" Dylan asked breathlessly.

"Amy's going to join up with Tybalt," Malory explained as they watched Amy lead Tybalt into the middle of the school. Tybalt walked steadily beside her, looking around with his ears pricked.

"Oh, so you're on a first-name basis now," Dylan joked. "Aren't you the aspiring horse healer?" Malory gave her a faint smile. "He looks calmer than I've ever seen him." Dylan whispered. "Did she drug him?"

Malory laughed and gave Dylan a shove. "No! We massaged him with lavender oil and sprayed this scent into the air. I know it sounds kooky, but T-touch really does work. Now shut up and watch."

Dylan leaned forward and gave her aunt a friendly

wave. Ali offered the girls a smile and then focused all of her attention on Tybalt and Amy in the ring.

Amy unclipped Tybalt's lunge line and stepped back. Tybalt tossed his head in the air and trotted away from her. Then he turned around, clearly confused when Amy didn't try to stop him.

"Go!" Amy called. She flicked the end of the rope at the pony's quarters.

Tybalt snorted and shied away. Malory bit her lip. Even though she had seen a demonstration of a join-up on film at the symposium, she was surprised by how harsh it seemed in real life.

"I want him to run away from me," Amy explained, as if she could tell how Malory was feeling. "I need him to think of me as being stronger, so I have to be firm."

Tybalt began to trot around the outside of the arena. Amy snapped the line, toward his hindquarters, and he broke into a canter. "He's a gorgeous mover," she commented.

Malory felt a rush of pride. It meant so much to her that Amy could see what she had spotted in Tybalt right from the start.

"So you're setting yourself up as the alpha horse," Ms. Carmichael commented.

Amy nodded, not taking her eyes off Tybalt. "In the wild a herd has one horse — usually the stallion — that the horses trust to be stronger than they are, and protect them when things get tough. I need to get Tybalt to put that same trust in me."

Malory had a feeling the explanation was for her benefit, and she took in every word. She lost count of how many times the brown gelding circled the arena. Whenever Amy stepped forward Tybalt slowed down, and when she stood back he sped up. Suddenly his hoofbeats slowed, and he dropped his head.

Malory grabbed Dylan's arm, nearly toppling off the fence. She motioned to Tybalt, who was opening and closing his mouth the same way the horse had in Amy's tutorial film.

"This is where you do the actual join-up, isn't it?" Malory called to Amy, who was watching Tybalt circle around her.

"He's telling me that he wants to stop running from me," Amy agreed. "Let's see what he does next."

Malory dug her nails into her palm. This was Tybalt's first chance to show he was willing to put his trust in people again!

Amy turned away from Tybalt so that she was no longer chasing him. The brown gelding slowed to a trot and then a walk. His inside ear swiveled toward Amy, and Malory could almost see his brain working as he tried to figure out what was going on. After a few more strides, Tybalt halted.

Dylan reached out and squeezed Malory's arm as Tybalt took a step away from the fence. He hesitated once more before walking over to Amy. When he was just a few feet away from her, Tybalt stopped. He stretched out his neck and blew against her back. Without looking around, Amy took a step forward.

Malory grinned when Tybalt walked forward, too, his neck still outstretched. Amy picked up her pace, and Tybalt trotted behind her around the ring. Amy led him on a trail of twists and turns until finally she stopped and rubbed his nose.

"If I hadn't seen it, I wouldn't believe it," Ms. Carmichael murmured.

Malory wanted to run out and hug both Tybalt and Amy when they headed to the gate side by side. But she knew this was just Tybalt's first step toward accepting people.

"I think he's lovely," Amy enthused, her cheeks flushed. "He's definitely looking for a chance to trust someone and start over."

"And you think after doing this with you, he'll respond positively when I put a rider on him?" Ms. Carmichael asked, running her hand down Tybalt's neck.

"Maybe not right away," Amy said. "He should have a few days with the remedies that I've given you, and with Malory doing T-touch. I'll come back on Sunday to join up with him again, and then maybe we could try a rider out."

Ms. Carmichael nodded. "It's really great of you to give your time like this." She smiled at Dylan and Malory. "I'm just glad these two came up with the idea to contact you."

Malory grinned at Dylan. "Great minds and all that."

Ms. Carmichael glanced at her watch. "I have a meeting to get to." She looked at Malory. "Will you take Tybalt back to his stall for me?"

"Sure." Malory nodded.

"I'd help, but I've got to go, too," Dylan said. "Lani and I have a study date." She smiled at Amy. "Thanks for letting me watch, Ms. Fleming. That was amazing."

"See you later." Amy raised her hand as Dylan and Ms. Carmichael walked across the arena. "I'll help you put Tybalt away," she offered to Malory.

"That would be great," Malory said warmly. She ran her fingers down Tybalt's damp neck, and the pony reached around to smell her hand. It might have been a small sign, but Malory considered it a good one.

🐦

Malory buckled Tybalt's blanket on while Amy filled his water bucket.

"I'm going to put some drops into this now," Amy explained, unscrewing the bottle of Bach Flower Remedy.

Malory gave Tybalt a pat before crossing the stall to

watch what Amy was doing. She was going to ask Ms. Carmichael if she could help with Tybalt's care for the next few days, and she wanted to pick up as many tips as she could.

She hesitated a moment, then took a deep breath. "There's something that's been bugging me for a while about Tybalt. Do you think that he's not used to being around other horses? I remember reading that horses who aren't socialized to other horses when they're young don't understand what it's like to live in a herd. I just figured that could be why Tybalt doesn't know how to act around other horses. Maybe he was brought up by himself — or even around cows — he seems to like them!"

Amy looked thoughtful. "That sounds like an interesting idea. It would explain why Tybalt hasn't bonded with the rest of the horses. Earning his trust will be a great way of helping him feel more at home here."

Malory felt her spirits rise; Amy had considered her theory, so maybe there was hope that Tybalt's attitude toward the other horses would improve. Malory went ahead and asked the other thing playing at her mind. "Is there any chance Tybalt could be ready for a competition at the end of next week?"

Amy raised her eyebrows. "Is that what you're aiming for?"

Malory reached up to check that Tybalt's hay net was securely tied. "The horse I usually ride is lame." She didn't want to tell Amy that Tybalt was responsible for Hardy's injury. "Ms. Carmichael's given me one of the new ponies to ride. Foxy's great, but I haven't clicked with her the way I think I could with Tybalt. I just have this feeling about him."

Amy nodded. "I know where you're coming from. I felt exactly the same about Sundance, the pony my mom gave me before she died. Even though we had lots of horses come to Heartland, I never bonded with any of them in the same way."

"Maybe you're just a one-pony girl," Malory suggested.

"I thought so for the longest time, but I have to admit that I'm kind of smitten with the horse you saw on the film in my talk," Amy admitted.

Malory thought back to the long-legged colt she'd seen Amy join up with. "Was that Spindleberry?"

Amy's face softened. "Yes, we rescued him from some pretty horrible conditions, and then my sister gave up some of her wedding money so we could buy Spindle and the horses that came with him. Now he's being trained using one-hundred-percent Heartland methods, and he seems to love every second of it."

"Heartland sounds like a paradise for horses," Malory said. "It must have been amazing growing up there!"

Amy's gray eyes sparkled. "I loved it. And I miss it when I'm at school." Amy was silent for a moment, but then her expression brightened. "But if I hadn't grown up at Heartland then I would have wanted to come to school *here*. It seems wonderful, and I'm excited to know that your trainer is open to various methods."

Malory grinned. She certainly wouldn't argue with that!

Amy went over to pat Tybalt. "I'll be back in a few days," she promised. "And then we'll see about you competing next week."

When Malory went to say good-bye, Tybalt stretched out his nose and snuffled her hair.

"It looks like the two of you are starting to bond." Amy smiled.

"I think he's fantastic," Malory admitted, gently pulling a strand of straw out of Tybalt's forelock.

"I think he's pretty terrific, too." Amy hesitated and met Malory's gaze straight on. "But that doesn't mean he's going to be cut out to be a riding-school horse. I'll do everything I can, Malory, but you're going to have to face the fact that Tybalt might be happier somewhere else."

CHAPTER TWELVE

It was Saturday, and Malory had already been to see Tybalt before brunch. To her delight, the dark brown gelding had nickered when she had gone into his stall, as if he was genuinely pleased to see her, not just expecting a tasty treat. She had worked on him with T-touch for a few minutes, and she could still smell the lavender oil on her fingers. The alternative treatments definitely seemed to be calming him down. Even Kelly had commented that Tybalt had been easier to bring in from the paddock over the last couple of days.

Now Malory was headed to the playing fields with Honey, Dylan, and Lani. Her friends were going to throw a softball, and Malory planned to catch up on her English reading — she hadn't been able to concentrate that week with the excitement of Amy Fleming's visit, so she was behind on the assignment Ms. Griffiths had given them.

Malory was in her own world as they walked, thinking

about Tybalt and how, most of all, she wanted him to be happy. But deep down, she hoped he would be happy at Chestnut Hill. Then Lani's voice broke her concentration.

"Whoa, another hockey practice? Ms. Feist sure isn't cutting Lynsey any slack." They stopped and stared at Lynsey, who was walking up the path toward them. She was wearing her short kiltlike skirt, and carrying her hockey stick over her shoulder.

Honey shook her head. "I don't know how she does it all."

"She must have a Lynsey clone," Dylan joked. "The real Lynsey Harrison is sprawled on a chaise longue somewhere, having a pedicure."

As Lynsey drew even with them, Malory noticed that her face was red and her hair clung damply to her forehead.

"Hey, Lynsey, we were just wondering if you'd managed to clone yourself," Lani grinned. "I don't know how you keep up with everything."

"It's called organization," Lynsey snapped. "It's not difficult for people who are sufficiently motivated." Malory was surprised to hear her be so defensive. Lani's comment had sounded relatively sympathetic.

Dylan raised an eyebrow. "What does that mean?"

"Go figure," Lynsey said. "I have to go. I've got a student council meeting in fifteen minutes."

"Oh, yes. Hurry along then!" Lani made a frantic motion with her hands and then frowned as Lynsey pushed past them even more rudely than usual.

In a way, Malory understood Lynsey's reaction. Why would she expect kindness from Lani or Dylan when they all made a point of giving one another a hard time? "I'll catch up with you guys in a minute," Malory called over her shoulder before jogging after Lynsey, who was hurrying toward the main campus.

Lynsey spun around to glare at her as she drew closer.

"Are you okay?" Malory panted.

Lynsey looked a little thrown. "My practice didn't go very well," she admitted, taking up a quick pace again across the lawn. "I let three balls get past me that I should have gotten easily."

"Maybe you're being too hard on yourself," Malory suggested. "You've only had a few practices with the team."

Lynsey shrugged. "The moment I start making excuses is the moment I sink to being average."

"Oh, we can't have you slumming with the rest of us." Malory smiled at her own joke, but Lynsey's expression didn't change. "Maybe you're just taking on too much," she suggested delicately.

Lynsey jerked to a stop. "And the reason I'd take Malory O'Neil's advice is what, exactly?" She tossed back her hair.

"Whenever anyone in my family takes on anything new, they always go straight to the top. So what would you know about what I can and can't do?" She turned on her heel. "Just do me a favor and leave me alone!"

Malory let her go. Lynsey always had to have the last word, and she obviously wasn't looking for an empathetic ear. *And I thought I had a lot to live up to, being the scholarship girl.* She shook her head. She wasn't feeling as intimidated by Lynsey as she used to. And she wasn't as annoyed by her attitude, either. *I've got it easy compared to being the youngest in a family of overachievers. It must be pretty lonely in Lynsey's world, with only enough room for one person at the top.*

🐾

On Sunday morning Malory went down to the yard extra early so she could spend time with Tybalt before Amy arrived. She got the remedy bottles from the feed room before heading to the barn. She looked in on Hardy first and was thrilled to see the chestnut pony up on his feet, pulling at his hay net. Dr. Olton had come out to see him the day before and had announced the gelding's leg was healing nicely. Malory had done a little victory dance outside Hardy's stable door. He still needed another seven weeks' rest, but knowing he was going to be okay was a huge relief.

When she looked over Tybalt's door, he blinked at her sleepily from where he was lying in the straw.

"Morning," Malory said softly, smiling as he scrambled up. He shook himself with a groan before walking forward to snuffle at her pockets.

"Here," she laughed, pulling out her last horse cookie. "We've got a lot to do this morning," she warned. "I want to make you look even more gorgeous before Amy comes to see you."

Tybalt crunched on the cookie and then looked past Malory's shoulder, his ears pricked. Malory turned in time to see Rose, the pony in the adjoining stall, push her velvety nose through the bars.

"You've made a friend!" she said in delight, as Tybalt reached up to blow into Rose's nostrils.

She unscrewed the top of the Bach Flower Remedy bottle and tipped a few drops onto her palm. Tybalt immediately dropped his head to graze his tongue over her hand.

Wiping her hand on a wad of straw, Malory took one of the other bottles and began to rub lavender oil into his coat, breathing in the sweet floral smell. She hoped it might relax her, too. Even though she was still delighted with the way it had gone with Tybalt on Amy's first visit, she couldn't help feeling he had a lot to live up to in today's session. Ms. Carmichael needed to be convinced that he was a reliable and safe ride before his future at

Chestnut Hill was assured. Malory stopped moving her fingertips in circles and twisted her oily fingers into Tybalt's mane.

"Please be good," she whispered, leaning her cheek against his warm neck.

☙

He looks amazing!" Amy commented.

Malory glanced up from picking out Tybalt's hoof. "Thanks! I really think he seems better."

"That's great." Amy unbolted the door and came in. "Ms. Carmichael had to take a phone call in her office. She asked if we'd meet her down at the arena."

"Okay," Malory said, putting the hoof pick into the grooming kit.

"I managed to trace some of Tybalt's history," Amy told her as they led the gelding out of his stall.

"Really? What did you find?"

"Mr. Ryan gave me the number of the auction house where he bought him. The people there wouldn't give me the number of Tybalt's previous owners, but they did pass my number on to them. They called me last night and said the reason they sold Tybalt was because whenever they rode him, he'd try to bolt back to the barn. They decided that the people who'd had him before had used a whip to teach him what they wanted in the ring. All it ended up teaching him was to run away from them. That would explain why he tenses up whenever he passes an entrance or gate. He's trying to make a break for it." Amy shrugged. "It's a good theory. I figure the more he ran, the more they hit him."

"Which made him want to run even more," Malory concluded, feeling her throat tighten.

Amy nodded. "And it also explains his fear of crops. His behavior's probably gotten worse with each new home because the owner's frustration with his attitude reinforced his fear. The people I talked to had hoped they could work through it, but their daughter was young and couldn't handle him."

Malory glanced at the pony walking beside her. *Poor Tybalt. No wonder he's so suspicious of everyone.*

"But I think we'll get through to him," Amy continued. "His previous owners said that when they first bought him, he had really liked to jump."

Malory felt her heart flip over. She knew it! She had sensed his potential the moment she first saw him!

Ms. Carmichael was waiting for them down at the ring. "It looks like Tybalt's got a fan base already," she commented.

Malory grinned when she saw Dylan, Lani, and Honey sitting on the fence. She knew they understood how important this session would be. Dylan waved vigorously, and Malory waved back, dropping her arm when Tybalt gave a startled snort.

"Sorry, boy," she apologized, rubbing his nose. "I didn't mean to scare you." She looked at Amy, hoping she wouldn't think Tybalt was too nervous to be ridden.

"Nothing changes overnight," Amy reassured her, as if she could read Malory's thoughts. "That's something I have to keep on learning at Heartland."

When they reached the center of the ring, Amy unclipped Tybalt's lunge line. "Over to you," she said, handing it to Malory.

Malory looked down at the line without taking it. "You want me to help?"

"Not just help," Amy replied, her gray eyes dancing. "I want you to join up with him!"

CHAPTER THIRTEEN

When Malory stared at her in astonishment, Amy smiled. "Ms. Carmichael agreed with me that you should. You're the one who's spent the most time with Tybalt."

From her place by the fence, Ms. Carmichael nodded. "He's going to respond better to you than anyone else."

"I can't!" Malory panicked. "I don't know what to do." But then she looked at Tybalt, who was watching her with his dark, intelligent eyes, and a feeling of excitement swept over her. Could she really persuade this gorgeous horse to trust her completely? She glanced over at her friends, who couldn't hear what was going on. *I'm going to join up with Tybalt!* she wanted to yell.

"I'll talk you through it every step of the way," Amy promised. "I'll stand right here. First, I need you to send Tybalt away from us, like I did last week."

Trying not to let her hands shake too much, Malory

took the coiled lunge line from Amy and flicked the rope at Tybalt's flank. He snorted in surprise and skittered away. Bracing herself, Malory flicked the line again, and he trotted to the fence, his ears flattened.

"Chasing him feels weird, I know," Amy told her, "especially after you've spent all this time trying to get close to him. But it's the only way to get him to accept that you're stronger than he is."

Malory nodded, too tense to speak. She watched Tybalt break into a canter with his tail kinked high.

"Keep driving him on. You're doing great," Amy encouraged.

Malory felt giddy as she spun on her heel to follow Tybalt's progress around the ring. Her friends were just a blur in the corner of her eye.

"Keep it up, Malory!" Ms. Carmichael called.

Malory smiled without taking her gaze off the dark brown gelding, who was eating up the ground with his long stride.

After one more circuit, Amy said, "Take a step forward into his line of vision to make him turn around."

Malory moved slightly ahead of Tybalt to block his action. At once the gelding wheeled around and cantered in the other direction, as smoothly as a fully trained dressage horse. Malory couldn't believe how much control she had over him without a lunge line or whip.

"Can you see his ear?" Amy murmured.

"The one that's pointing inward?" Malory asked.

"Yes. That means he's ready to join up with us," Amy told her.

"What do we do now?"

"Keep him going for a little while longer," Amy replied. "We want him to be absolutely confident about his decision."

Malory watched Tybalt until he dropped his head down, and began opening and closing his mouth.

"Now turn your shoulder side on to him and drop your eye contact," Amy said.

Malory twisted away, showing Tybalt that she no longer wanted to chase him around the ring. She had always known instinctively that this was a nonthreatening position — after he had thrown Lynsey in the indoor ring, she had backed her way to him. She could just see him out of the corner of her eye. He had slowed to a stop and was looking in their direction.

"When he comes up to you, I want you to walk forward a few steps, okay?" Amy whispered.

Malory waited, feeling the hairs on her neck stand up when she heard the quiet thud of hooves on the sand.

"Now," Amy said quietly.

Malory's heart thudded as she stepped forward. She couldn't believe that Tybalt would actually follow her. But a second later a soft nose bumped into her shoulder. Malory turned around and looked into Tybalt's dark brown eyes. They were filled with trust, with no hint of the fear and anxiety that had troubled him since his arrival.

She reached up and wrapped her arms around his neck. *We did it,* she thought. *We really did it!*

She looked up at the sound of cheers from the far side of the arena. Lani, Honey, and Dylan were doing what Malory guessed was the wave. It didn't look very impressive with only three people, but it meant the world to Malory. She smiled at them, then turned back to Amy.

"Thank you," she said, meaning it with her whole heart.

Amy nodded, and somehow Malory knew without her saying anything that she understood how much this moment meant to her. *It must be totally amazing to do join-ups all the time.*

Malory pressed her cheek against Tybalt's neck. "You did great," she told him. But she knew that they still had to test Tybalt's trust. "Are you going to ride him now?" she asked Amy.

Amy paused. "It's usually best if the person who did the join-up rides first."

Malory glanced at Ms. Carmichael.

Ms. Carmichael came over and reached out to rub Tybalt between the eyes. "It's a good idea to try him out while he's behaving so well," she agreed. "But I don't want to take too many chances. He's still unpredictable."

"I'll keep a close eye on him," Amy promised.

Ms. Carmichael called across to ask Dylan to get Tybalt's tack.

Lani cupped her hands and shouted, "We're rooting for you! Good luck!"

I hope I don't need luck, Malory thought. *I've got trust working for me this time around.*

🐃

Ready?" Amy held Tybalt's reins and smiled at Malory, who was fastening her chinstrap.

"Ready," Malory said. She put her foot into the stirrup and swung up onto Tybalt's back. "We're going to take a walk around the arena, and you're going to just relax, okay?" she told him.

Tybalt's ear flicked back.

"Take it steady," Ms. Carmichael warned.

Malory nodded as she took up her reins. She hadn't even been this nervous at the demonstration! But back then only her scholarship had been at stake; somehow that didn't compare with Tybalt's entire future at Chestnut Hill.

"Go, girl!" Dylan called from the fence where she, Honey, and Lani were sitting with their fingers crossed.

Tybalt lowered his head and started to walk down the arena.

"Ask him for a trot," Ms. Carmichael called.

Malory felt a rush of adrenaline as she shortened her reins. Tybalt snatched at the bit and rushed forward.

"Try again," Amy advised. "Pretend you're riding the best-trained pony ever. You set the standard and then ride like you expect him to meet it."

Malory nodded. That made sense. She brought Tybalt's hocks under him with a half-halt and asked him to trot again.

This time Tybalt broke into a smooth trot, carrying Malory effortlessly across the sand with long, floating strides. *This can't be happening! He feels like a totally different horse.* At the end of the arena, she turned to trot down the diagonal. All of the time she felt Tybalt listening to what she was asking him to do, putting his trust in her instead of fighting against what she wanted. Halfway down she sat for a stride to change the diagonal, noticing that Tybalt didn't falter in his pace.

"Good boy," she whispered.

At the next corner, she asked him to canter. Tybalt's dark mane whipped back over her hands as he lengthened his stride. "Steady, boy." Malory laughed, bringing him back to a trot at the end of the arena.

She rode Tybalt in a serpentine, pleased at the way he worked steadily through each loop until she brought him to a halt. It was clear that at some point in his checkered history, he'd been well schooled. And Amy's tip about expecting the best from him worked wonders — she just had to believe that Tybalt was willing to do exactly what she asked.

The others waited for Malory to drop her stirrups and slip down from Tybalt before breaking into cheers.

"You were amazing!" Dylan called over the fence.

"He certainly wanted to do his best for you," Ms. Carmichael agreed.

"He looked like a different horse," Honey enthused.

"He felt like one, too," Malory admitted. "Thanks to Amy."

"Let's call it a team effort." Amy smiled, taking Tybalt's reins over his head.

Malory turned to Ms. Carmichael. "What did you think of him?"

"I think you rode him very well," Ali Carmichael told her. She pulled out a section of Tybalt's forelock that was trapped under his brow band. "But I can't be totally sure he'll cut it as a school pony. One smooth ride's not a guarantee of his behavior. He's going to need a lot of patience and commitment."

"I can do that," Malory jumped in. There was no way she was giving up now! A blue ribbon at the Saint Kits show seemed so close, she just had to reach out to touch it. "That is, if it's okay with you, Ms. Carmichael?"

Ms. Carmichael smiled. "Let's put it this way, Tybalt's definitely earned a chance to prove himself."

"Does this mean I can take him in the lesson tomorrow?" Malory persisted.

Ms. Carmichael raised her hands. "I can't really say no after that performance!"

Malory looked at Amy and grinned. "I owe you," she mouthed.

Amy shook her head. "Nothing's better than helping a horse work through the problems from his past and start over. That's all the thanks I need. But I do ask that you take it slow. Let him ease into everything."

Malory nodded. She wouldn't push him. It wasn't worth it.

As Amy walked away with Ms. Carmichael, Malory's friends rushed into the ring. Dylan and Lani enveloped her in a delighted hug.

"You're like a miracle worker," Honey said, holding her hand out for Tybalt to sniff.

"No, it was all Tybalt," Lani said. "He's the brave one for putting trust in Malory. What was he thinking?"

Malory rolled her eyes, feigning exasperation.

"I'm not so sure," Dylan said, sounding surprisingly earnest. "I think Tybalt finally has it right. Don't you, boy?"

Malory smiled, and the four of them walked the pony to the barn.

❧

Lynsey turned in the saddle and snapped, "Make sure you keep that animal away from Bluegrass."

Malory half-halted Tybalt so there was more distance between the two ponies. Malory wasn't going to make a scene in the middle of class, but Lynsey wasn't being fair. Tybalt had worked really well during the exercises on the flat, and Malory couldn't wait to see how he went over the jumps.

Malory watched Bluegrass trot over the poles Ms. Carmichael had set out for them at the top end of the arena.

"Steady," she murmured when Tybalt tossed his head, eager to follow. Her mouth felt dry, and she tried to make herself relax, knowing that Tybalt would pick up on her nerves. *If only I had some lavender oil to rub on me!* she thought, forcing herself to take deep breaths. Once the roan was halfway over the poles, she let Tybalt go, hoping that his good behavior on the flat wouldn't vanish. She kept her eyes on the small cross pole at the end that they had to jump over.

Tybalt's stride faltered on the last pole before the jump. Malory closed her legs to balance him and drove him forward over the fence. Tybalt snorted as he rose into the air and then cantered to join the rest of the class.

"Way to go." Dylan took one hand off Morello's reins to give Malory a thumbs-up.

"Thanks," Malory puffed, patting Tybalt's neck. *First obstacle successfully cleared, in more ways than one!*

"Bring them into the center," Ms. Carmichael called. "Except for Tybalt. I'd like him to take the course first, please."

Malory shortened her reins as Tybalt tried to follow the other horses. She had walked the course at the start of the class to pace the distances between the six jumps, and had ridden it in her mind at least a dozen times, always with Tybalt soaring clear over every fence. Now that she was about to ride it for real, she felt butterflies take up camp in her gut, and her hands felt clammy inside her gloves.

She trotted Tybalt in a circle to settle him before turning him toward the first fence. His head shot up, and his stride went choppy when he caught sight of the upright. Malory circled him away from the fence to calm him down.

"Come on, boy," she said, turning him at the fence again. "Trust me."

Tybalt pricked his ears, and this time his gait stayed smooth as he cantered up to the rail. He sprang into the air, almost making Malory gasp as she felt the power of his hindquarters. He was as amazing as she had imagined he would be! The moment they landed she turned him to the parallel bars, keeping her legs on the girth so Tybalt knew she was with him every inch of the way.

Tybalt gathered himself before the jump and sailed over the rails. *He's really enjoying himself,* Malory realized with delight.

They cleared the bars with inches to spare. Malory made sure she didn't drop the contact with him as they flew over the wall and the spread. Then she turned him toward the final fence, another upright with a small wading pool underneath, complete with floating rubber ducks. Malory knew Ms. Carmichael put it up because she wanted the horses to be prepared for any unexpected fence decorations in the course at Saint Kits on Wednesday.

Tybalt's stride faltered. He pulled to the right, and Malory increased her contact on the left rein with her right leg hard on the girth. *Don't do that to me! You can't run out on the last one!*

Almost like he understood how important it was, Tybalt straightened out and sailed into the air at the last second. The pole made a threatening rattle, and Malory was sure that it would fly off its holder. But when they landed and the rest of the class went wild with whoops and applause, she realized they had gone clear.

She ran her hand down his neck. "Good boy!"

"That was unreal!" Dylan called.

"Does this mean Malory gets to ride Tybalt for the show on Wednesday?" Lani asked.

Before Ms. Carmichael could answer, Lynsey spoke up. "You can't possibly take a horse as unpredictable as that to the Saint Kits show. If he freaks out, what will that say about Chestnut Hill?"

Ms. Carmichael frowned. "I'll be the one to decide which horses will represent Chestnut Hill, and I will consider all of the factors. Thank you, Lynsey."

Lynsey opened her mouth to argue, but Ms. Carmichael held up her hand. "Honey, I'd like you to ride next, please."

After everyone had jumped the course once, Ms. Carmichael ended the lesson. "Please stay behind, Malory."

As soon as the arena had emptied, Ms. Carmichael walked over. "I'd like you to keep your place on the team for the show this Wednesday," she said. "You've worked very hard with Tybalt, and you deserve it."

"You're letting me enter on Tybalt?" Malory felt her spirits soar.

"Hold on." Ms. Carmichael placed her hand on Tybalt's neck. "I'm interested in seeing how Tybalt reacts to the pressure of a show ground, but I'm not convinced he's ready to compete. It might even be too early to determine if he can handle it, but it's just a practice show, so we have nothing to lose."

Malory felt her spirits plummet.

Nothing to lose? Malory felt like she had everything to lose. She knew that this show was a friendly competition, organized to give the junior teams a chance to warm up for the All Schools League, but this would be the only chance she'd have to prove Tybalt was up to the challenge.

"We'll be sending five horses," Ms. Carmichael explained, "but we only need four to complete the course."

Malory frowned. "I'm confused. Are we going to get to compete?"

"Yes, as long as Tybalt looks like he can handle being on a show ground. I think the show will be a great test of how he copes with pressure. But if you get a sense that it's just too much for him, then I'm trusting you to pull out. We don't want a setback, but we do need to be making a decision."

Malory bit her lip. She had hoped that Ms. Carmichael was going to give her a final decision about Tybalt's future at Chestnut Hill today, but she knew that her proposed plan was fair. After all, Tybalt had a lot to prove after his earlier outbursts. *So everything is riding on the show.* And he may have jumped like a dream today, but a noisy, packed show ground would be a very different environment. She ran her hand down Tybalt's mane as they walked out of the ring.

She still believed he was a champion in the making, but now she needed him to believe it, too.

CHAPTER FOURTEEN

Malory turned around in her seat, peering at the goose-neck of the horse trailer hitched to the truck.

"That's the tenth time you've done that, and we're only halfway there," Dylan teased. "You can't see anything anyway."

Malory turned back around. "I'm just worried Tybalt might think he's getting shipped to another new home."

"Hey, only positive thoughts allowed," warned George, one of the grounds staff. He was driving the junior team horses over to Saint Kits with Dylan and Malory. The rest of the team was following behind with Ms. Carmichael.

"You've got it. No negative vibes for the rest of the trip. I promise," Malory said, but she instinctively went to turn her head. She shouted with laughter as Dylan elbowed her in the side.

"Thank goodness Saint Kits is only on the other side

of town. You'd get a permanent kink in your neck if you were stuck in here any longer," Dylan said.

Malory pushed her shoulders back and stared straight ahead. "If you see me turn, you have my permission to wring my neck."

"But how would you represent Chestnut Hill in a neck brace?" Dylan teased. "That wouldn't look good for the school."

Malory tried to laugh, but it came out more like a hic-cup. Suddenly she was fully aware that she was riding for Chestnut Hill — not just for herself or even for Tybalt. Good or bad, their ride would reflect on the school as well.

You won't believe the course!" Lani hurried up with Honey only a few paces behind.

"It's a total nightmare." They'd arrived ahead of the riders. The Chestnut Hill van had brought a load of fans for the day's event, and Lani had obviously made good use of her extra time on the grounds.

"Thank you for your opinion, Lani. I'm planning on walking the course with the team now," said Ms. Carmichael. "Would you mind staying here to help George keep an eye on the horses?"

"Sure thing," Lani said. The team ponies were tied to

the side of the trailer with lead lines. The girls had groomed and braided the ponies before leaving and had just put their saddles on their backs. "Do you want us to put their galloping boots on?"

Ms. Carmichael nodded. "We'll be back as soon as we can to help."

As the Chestnut Hill riders walked across the paddock toward the huge indoor arena, the Allbrights junior team passed them going the other way. They looked ultraconfident in their burgundy team sweatshirts and white jodhs.

Ms. Carmichael smiled at the instructor. "Hello, Elizabeth."

Malory looked curiously at the tall auburn-haired woman walking at the head of the Allbrights team. *That must be the famous Elizabeth Mitchell!* Malory examined the trainer who had led Chestnut Hill to the league championship last year, only to leave for a position at the rival school. *If she had stayed at Chestnut Hill, would I be here?* There was no way of knowing if Ms. Mitchell would have supported Diane Rockwell's decision to give her a scholarship. And, if what Lynsey said was true, she certainly wouldn't have given Tybalt the second and third chances he had needed to make it to the show.

"Watch your pace between fences four and five," Ms. Mitchell was saying to her students, slapping a crop against the top of her black riding boot. "The distance is deceptive." She broke off to nod at Ms. Carmichael before carrying on.

The Saint Kits arena was larger than the one at Chestnut Hill. Malory liked the fact it had an under-cover collecting ring with a practice jump for warming up. The team skirted around the outside of the stadium, heading for the entrance that led into the main arena. Malory paused in the doorway to look around. Smooth yellow sand seemed to stretch away forever, dotted with freshly painted fences and tubs of flowers. At the far end was a window to an observation room. The rest of the arena was surrounded by rows and rows of bleachers behind a clear plastic screen.

Dylan nudged her. "I see what Lani meant about the course."

Malory followed her gaze and gulped. The fences looked a lot more substantial than the ones they schooled over. More impressive and more intimidating. She glanced sideways at Lynsey, who was fiddling with her gloves and not saying anything for once. *If Lynsey's nervous then I'm in trouble!*

"Come on, team. There's nothing here you haven't tackled before," Ms. Carmichael said briskly.

They walked up to the first fence along the outside wall. "This shouldn't give you any trouble, as long as you've got enough momentum," their instructor told them. "Your horse is going to size up the back pole as the highest point, so he should clear the lower pole without a problem."

The girls nodded. Suddenly they all seemed too stunned to speak. They walked over to the parallel bars, their feet sending up small clouds of sand.

"You've jumped these a million times in practice," said Ms. Carmichael. "You just need to make sure that you get your takeoff right. If you get too close, you'll take down the front pole." She rested her hand on the red-and-white bar. "Too late, and your pony will be flat. Then he'll snag it with his hind legs."

The next fence was a triple bar. "Shamrock hates these," Olivia moaned.

"You need to make sure she lengthens her stride well before the fence. Don't wait until the last few strides," Ms. Carmichael advised.

Malory looked at the row of brightly colored plants along the base of the fence and made a mental note: She'd have to keep Tybalt totally between her hands and legs or else all the decorations could spook him. Every jump had some filler or a flag. The ring was full of distractions!

They turned and walked over to the gate in the middle of the course. "Just tackle this the same as any upright," Ms. Carmichael told them. "Malory, sometimes you try too hard. You don't need to lift your horse over!"

Malory smiled. She knew she'd struggled a few times in practice lately over the higher uprights. But she wouldn't have to worry about that with Tybalt. Most of the time it felt as if he had springs for hindlegs!

"This spread is wide. You need your takeoff here to clear it." Ms. Carmichael kicked at the sand with her toe. "And make sure you are straight in the saddle — your horse needs you to stay balanced!"

Malory concentrated hard on remembering everything. This was the most demanding course she'd seen, never mind jumped. *And Tybalt and I still have everything to prove.*

🐎

Here." Honey threw Malory a can of soda. Ms. Carmichael had sent her over to the café at the back of the indoor arena to get drinks for everyone.

"Can you hold on to it for me?" Malory asked, tossing it back. "I'm about to go warm Tybalt up over the practice jump."

"Sure," Honey said. "Do you want me to come with you and pick up poles?" She quickly checked herself. "Not that you're going to knock any down, of course."

"That would be great." Malory smiled, trying to ignore the tension knotting in her stomach. She reached up to untie Tybalt from the side of the trailer. Lynsey had insisted that Bluegrass should be kept on the other side, even though Tybalt had been fine with all the other horses. His socialization issues had definitely been resolved, thanks to Amy's advice, and thanks to getting used to life in the busy barn.

"He looks amazing," Honey said admiringly.

Malory stood back for a second to appreciate the way Tybalt's dark coat gleamed in the autumn sun. His black mane was sewn and tied into neat braids, and his tail had been pulled into a French-style braid with black yarn at the bottom. Malory had spent ages the night before polishing his tack, which was set off gorgeously by the white saddlepad with the navy Chestnut Hill logo in each corner.

She heard a low whistle and turned to see a couple of girls walking by wearing hunter-green team shirts. They were both looking at Tybalt. "He's gorgeous! I wonder if he's got Thoroughbred in him. Or some Warmblood."

Malory basked in their appreciative comments, remembering the first time she had seen him. They had come so far, yet they still had a long way to go before they were in the clear.

"Nervous?" Eleanor asked as she untied Skylark.

"Are you kidding? You heard what those girls said just now. If he jumps as good as he looks, we're set," Malory joked.

She mounted Tybalt, thinking briefly of Hardy back at home who was missing out on all this. Part of her would have loved to be riding the reliable cob right now. Tybalt swung his head around and nibbled at her boot. Malory grinned. Even though Hardy would have been the easier ride, it didn't mean she regretted being here with Tybalt for one moment. "Come on, boy," she said.

The field behind the arena where all of the trailers were parked was pulsing with activity as team members mounted and began to warm up. Malory looked around for Caleb, wondering if he was on the Saint Kits team. She shook her head. *Duh!* Of course the Saint Kits team wouldn't be out on the field. They'd be getting tacked up in their stable. Malory glanced at the beautiful old stone wall that separated the stable yard from the rest of the facilities. There was something about the campus, with its ivy-covered masonry, that felt so classic. The buildings, the ring, and even the concession stand seemed high class. She wasn't at a local show with a taped-off outdoor ring anymore. This was the real thing.

"Looking for anyone special?" Dylan teased, riding up beside her on Morello.

"Huh?" Malory looked across at her friend, who was grinning.

"Is Caleb on the Saint Kits team, by any chance?" Dylan prompted.

"I don't know! He's a good rider, but I don't know if he even tried out," Malory told her. "And I don't know why you think I was looking for him, considering he's someone else's boyfriend. I'm just checking out the competition."

There were five other teams taking part, and even though Ms. Carmichael had reassured them over and over that it was just a friendly competition, the atmosphere was still tense. The same teams would be up against one another in the All Schools League, so it was difficult to remember that no points were being recorded for this event.

The Allbrights team had taken over a section at the back of the field.

"They look really good," Malory murmured as two of the girls struck off in a perfect collected canter side by side.

"And so do we," Dylan told her.

Malory tried to smile. She appreciated Dylan's reassurance, but she still felt enormous pressure. She was riding to prove that Tybalt deserved to stay at Chestnut Hill — and that her instincts had been right.

"Why is Patience hanging around the arena entrance?" she asked, trying to relax into Tybalt's stride. The Chestnut Hill supporters were supposed to be in the viewing area. Patience looked totally out of place standing there in a Versace skirt and a short-sleeved cashmere sweater.

"It doesn't take a genius to figure out that she must

be waiting for a certain rider from Saint Kits," Dylan commented. "Which must mean Caleb *did* make the team."

"Right." Malory pushed away the increasingly familiar stab of disappointment at the thought of Caleb and Patience together. She concentrated instead on being pleased that Caleb made the team. He'd talked to her in the summer about how much he'd wanted to represent Saint Kits. *And I represent Chestnut Hill. That means we'll be competing against each other!*

There was a line of riders inside the collecting ring, waiting to go over the practice fence. Two Saint Kits boys wearing yellow steward vests were standing on either side of the jump, ready to pick up the poles if they fell. Malory didn't join the back of the line. She wanted to keep Tybalt on his own as much as possible. He was comfortable with his stablemates now, but she didn't want to put him under unnecessary pressure.

Instead she rode him over to a quiet spot and began to trot him in a figure eight. She kept glancing over to the practice jump; and the moment there was a gap, she pushed Tybalt into a canter. She drove him strongly toward the jump and felt a rush of delight as he leaped over.

"He seems to be in a good mood!" Honey called as Malory trotted back to her and Dylan. Morello pawed the ground like he couldn't wait to go next.

"Let's hope it lasts," Malory replied, reining him to a halt as the rest of the Chestnut Hill team approached.

Eleanor Dixon rode over to her on Skylark. The chestnut mare snorted, arching her neck and swishing her tail, clearly enjoying the buzz of the show ground. It was one of the key reasons Skylark had been such a standout in competitions. Showing off in the ring came naturally to her.

Malory ran her eye over the rest of the team ponies, which looked fabulous, every bit as good as the other teams' horses. Olivia Buckley had Shamrock standing quietly, which wasn't as easy as she made it look. The blue-gray mare was one of the most high-spirited rides at Chestnut Hill. Bluegrass, as usual, looked like a model pony. He played with his bit as Lynsey assessed the competition.

Malory felt Tybalt shift uneasily underneath her, and she brought her attention back to him. Most of the riders were collecting in groups around their riding instructors, so the practice jump was free. Malory shortened her reins and directed Tybalt to the fence a second time, hoping to keep him composed. But Tybalt took off too soon and gave a huge leap to compensate. Thrown off balance, Malory grabbed a handful of mane as he landed. When he felt the reins go slack, Tybalt exploded forward.

Malory hurried to tighten her grip, trying to pull him back, but Tybalt was out of control and swerved into the path of a gray horse that was being ridden past. Tybalt laid his ears back and squealed, swinging his hindquarters around at the horse.

"Steady!" Malory called desperately, sensing he was about to bolt.

As the rider of the gray tried to pull his horse away, Tybalt reared up. Malory dropped her weight forward and waited for him to pitch back forward.

It felt like an eternity that Malory held on and prayed Tybalt wouldn't fall backward. She was aware of the other rider leaping off his horse and grabbing Tybalt's bridle. "Easy, there, easy!"

Tybalt dropped down to the sand. He was trembling, and as Malory smoothed his neck she could feel him breaking out into a sweat.

"Are you okay?" The rider glanced up at her, his blue eyes wide with concern.

Malory felt her face turn scarlet underneath her hard hat. Why did Caleb always have to appear at the wrong moment?

"Caleb, I'm so sorry. H-he can be unpredictable around other horses," she stammered, glad to see one of the stewards holding Caleb's horse a few feet away. "He's still got a lot to figure out."

Ms. Carmichael ran over, looking worried. "What happened?"

"He overjumped the practice fence; and before I could

reel him in, he almost collided with another horse," Malory said. "Then he just came undone."

"If you're okay, I'd better get back to my horse," Caleb interrupted, flashing Malory a quick smile.

"Sure, thanks," she called as he walked away.

Ms. Carmichael frowned. "Well, what do you think? Do you still want to do the practice round?"

"Absolutely." Malory nodded, ignoring her racing pulse. This was her chance to show that Tybalt was worthy of a place at Chestnut Hill. The practice round was a lower, shorter version of the main course, and it wasn't part of the competition so there would be only a fraction of the pressure.

"He still looks pretty uptight to me, but you know him better than anyone else," Ms. Carmichael said. She ran her hand down Tybalt's shoulder. "I trust you to scratch the moment he starts to act up — we'll still have four riders."

Malory nodded as Ms. Carmichael led Tybalt over to the rest of the team. She wondered if the others felt as nervous about her performance as she did. At least if you screwed up when you were on your own, you weren't responsible for letting four other people down.

From his back, Malory could see that Tybalt's nostrils still flared with each breath. He snorted and began to paw at the ground.

"Oh great, he's about to flip again," Lynsey said, pulling Bluegrass away.

When Malory's name was called, she felt a rush of nerves that left her feeling dizzy.

"Don't forget, you're just jumping four fences. Numbers one, two, five, and eight," Ms. Carmichael said, standing back from Tybalt. "Good luck!"

"Go, Malory!" called Olivia and Eleanor.

Malory tightened her chinstrap and rode toward the massive doors. Beneath her, Tybalt yanked at the reins, picking up on her nerves.

Dylan was standing by the entrance on Morello. "Good luck," she called as Malory rode by.

Malory was too anxious to reply. She touched the school crest on her fleece jacket once for luck, then shortened her reins. As they trotted into the center of the arena, she tried to block out the mass of faces thronging the ringside. *Just think about Tybalt,* she told herself, pushing the gelding into a canter.

Tybalt's stride felt choppy, and Malory realized he was on the wrong lead. She circled him again and crossed the starting line.

Tybalt seemed to go in slow motion as they approached the first fence. Then everything sprang to fast forward as he flew over the jump with confidence.

Clear! Malory had to hold the gelding back to stop him from rushing the parallel bars. Tybalt was fighting her hands, not wanting to listen to her signals. *Trust me,* Malory begged him silently, giving and taking on the reins to get his attention. Tybalt took off much too close, and the crowd groaned as the top bar clattered onto the sand. The noise upset Tybalt. He shook his head, pulling Malory forward out of the saddle.

Malory knew she needed to settle him quickly, so she cantered him straight past fence five, keeping her hands and legs as still as she could. She circled him around and gave him a straighter shot at fence number five. Tybalt took a huge leap, landing with a long stride. Malory squeeze-released with the reins, but Tybalt wouldn't slow down. They were only four strides from the next fence, but Malory knew that if they kept going, he'd bring the whole fence down. There was no way she was going to risk hurting him just to make her point. She pulled on the right rein and he swerved away from the fence, slowly evening his pace and lowering his head.

Malory bit her lip. She just had to accept that Tybalt wasn't ready to compete as a member of the team. She didn't want to end their round on such a disastrous note, so she angled him toward the first fence again. With a snort Tybalt launched into the air and landed cleanly on the other side. Malory brought him back to a trot, and completed a circle. Even though the arena burst into applause, she felt choked with disappointment. She had let Ms. Carmichael and Chestnut Hill down, but worst of all, she knew Tybalt's future had been decided.

CHAPTER FIFTEEN

Malory trotted back to the collecting ring, passing Dylan and Ms. Carmichael. She felt too miserable to talk to them now.

Lynsey cut across her on Bluegrass, forcing her to pull up. "Way to go, Malory. You missed two fences. Exactly when are you going to start showing this incredible talent that got you the Rockwell grant?"

Malory stared straight ahead, determined not to let Lynsey get to her.

"You should never have brought that pony here in the first place. Of all people, I thought you knew better," Lynsey continued, her voice bitter.

"Can it, Lynsey!" Dylan demanded, riding up. "We're supposed to be a team, which means we support one another no matter what. You don't hear any of us scolding you for missing practice sessions so you can play field hockey."

"That's because you know you can count on me for a solid ride," Lynsey retorted. "You'd think we could rely on the scholarship girl for that, too. But no, she has to ride an emotional wreck of a pony just because she feels sorry for him."

Malory couldn't think of anything to say. She didn't feel sorry for Tybalt. She believed in him, but what had that really gotten her — or him for that matter? She pulled her left rein and steered Tybalt around Bluegrass, heading away from the rest of her team.

"Good work, Malory!" Ms. Carmichael appeared beside her. "No one watching would have believed that you'd had only a few days' practice. Or that he wouldn't even trot a week ago."

Malory flinched. Was Ms. Carmichael trying to rub it in? How could she congratulate her on that ride?

The riding instructor reached up to pat the gelding's damp neck. "I know you're disappointed with the way he went. There were some significant communication issues. But you rode him just right. You were firm but understanding all the way."

Malory bit her lip. This wasn't what she wanted to hear. It was great that Ms. Carmichael was pleased with the way she'd ridden, but the Director of Riding was obviously less than impressed with Tybalt's behavior.

"Maybe if I'd started at a slower pace, he'd have gone better," she said. "Or maybe I just didn't read him right."

Ms. Carmichael frowned. "I have no idea what you're talking about. You've gotten more out of Tybalt than anyone else could have, especially after the scene at the practice jump. You gave him everything you could. The only thing he needed more of is time. He's still inexperienced. With a little more practice, he'll know just what to do. It's obvious that he trusts you." She looked hard at Malory until she met her instructor's gaze. "You know, Diane Rockwell didn't give you a scholarship because you won blue ribbons. She liked how you relate to horses and understand them. She wanted to foster your instinct, and I know she'd be proud of what you've done with this guy." Ali Carmichael rubbed the pony's muzzle.

"But I've still blown it, right?" Malory pointed out. "I mean, I know I shouldn't take him for the full course, so what does that mean? His trial is almost up."

Ali Carmichael sighed. "The team jumping's about to begin. We'll talk about Tybalt later, okay?"

As her instructor walked away, Malory dropped her stirrups and jumped down from Tybalt. She couldn't bear the thought of the beautiful horse being sent back. She leaned against his shoulder, feeling his warmth and solidness. *Oh, Tybalt!* Saying good-bye to Zanzibar had been terrible, but this was far, far worse. She couldn't help feeling responsible for the way things had gone. If she hadn't jumped the practice fence and almost collided with Caleb, would everything be different now?

Malory slipped Tybalt's reins over his head and loosened his girth before leading him over to the rest of the team. What Dylan had said about them all supporting one another was true — and that meant she couldn't go off and sulk in a corner even though she was out of the competition.

"Olivia, you're up first," Ms. Carmichael called.

Olivia nodded, shortening her reins. As her name was announced over the loudspeaker, she smiled tensely. "Wish me luck."

"Good luck," Malory yelled with the others as Olivia trotted toward the entrance.

Dylan nudged Morello closer. The paint gelding looked stunning, his white splotches gleaming. "Are you okay? You handled him really well, you know. He looked like he was on the verge of freaking out, but you managed to keep him together."

"Thanks. I feel like I totally screwed up," Malory said.

"Not from where I was standing," Dylan reassured her. "The horse can really jump. I think that in a few weeks, you'll have him going like a dream."

"I don't think Ms. Carmichael's going to give us that long," Malory said, feeling a stab of pain. She looked down and fiddled with her glove, relieved that Dylan didn't push the subject further.

Their attention was suddenly taken by Olivia, who was trotting out of the arena.

Malory strained to listen to the announcement over the sound of cheers from the arena: *Olivia Buckley goes clear on Shamrock for Chestnut Hill.*

Yay! Malory felt a rush of pride on Olivia's behalf.

Kathleen Orwen from Wycliffe Academy was called next. The girl on the palomino trotted past Malory, looking determined.

Three more riders went before Lynsey was called. *Lynsey going clear is a given,* Malory thought. Dylan and Eleanor Dixon broke away to trot Morello and Skylark in small circles to keep them focused.

When Lynsey rode out a few minutes later, the girls halted to listen to the loudspeaker: *Lynsey Harrison riding for Chestnut Hill on Bluegrass, six faults.*

Malory swapped a surprised look with Dylan, wondering if she had heard wrong. But when she looked at Lynsey's pale face, she realized that the pressure was really on Dylan and Eleanor to go clear.

"What happened?" Eleanor called as Lynsey rode by.

"I got six faults, that's what happened," Lynsey replied tightly.

Allbrights had had two clear rounds so far and were in the lead. Eleanor was the next Chestnut Hill rider to go.

"She'll be fine," Olivia assured everyone. But Malory noticed that Eleanor's fingers were gripping her reins so hard her knuckles had gone white.

A groan came from the arena. A minute later Eleanor came riding out, shaking her head. "I totally screwed up on the combination," she said.

So it's all on Dylan, Malory thought, her stomach twisting itself into knots. Normally Dylan would be the reserve rider, and they'd only count her points if they were better than the other scores. But since Malory had scratched, Dylan's points counted no matter what.

Tybalt, picking up on Malory's tension, pawed at the ground. "Steady," Malory murmured, stroking his neck.

When Dylan's name was called, Malory followed her to the main ring entrance. "Good luck," she said, her voice lost in the burst of applause as Dylan trotted into the huge arena.

Malory put her hand on Tybalt's neck, hoping he'd stay still, and watched as her friend cantered a circle. When Morello took the first jump, he made it look easy, his ears pricked forward as he looked toward his next fence.

Dylan rode him strongly over the parallel bars and then sent him on to the triple bar. *Focus on the middle pole,* Malory willed her, remembering Ms. Carmichael's earlier advice. It looked like Dylan remembered, too, as Morello took off at just the right moment to sail over the fence. The gate was next. Malory felt that for the first time Morello's attention wasn't one hundred percent, as he strayed off the line Dylan had taken for their approach. Dylan straightened him out by using her left leg; and Malory held her breath as they cantered at the upright, taking off with plenty of room to spare. They landed clear, and Morello raced on.

The next fence was a stile — and what was worse, it was a vertical pole straight after a corner, which always unsettled Morello. He began to drop away from the fence, and Malory saw Dylan sit deep to drive him on. Although he jumped in time, Malory knew they didn't have enough height to clear it. She wasn't surprised when he sent the top pole flying. *Come on, Dylan. Help him focus!*

Morello gave a huge jump over the next fence before racing on to the combination. "Too fast," Malory murmured, tightening her fingers unconsciously on Tybalt's rein. Dylan half-halted Morello, and the gelding collected himself for the first of the combination fences. They landed perfectly on the other side of the first fence. Dylan sat tight for his bounce stride to take him up and over the second fence. They flew over and raced through the finish. *Only four faults!*

"Go, Dylan!" Malory would have leaped into the air, but she didn't want to frighten Tybalt. Even though there was too much of a gap for the Chestnut Hill team to catch up with the leaders, it was fantastic that Dylan had turned in such a strong performance. She had brought some of the feel-good factor back to the afternoon.

🐾

After they had settled the ponies in the trailer, Malory and Dylan went back to join Honey and Lani for the end of the competition. The Allbrights team was now so far in the lead they were unbeatable. Wycliffe and Saint Kits were battling for second place. Chestnut Hill wasn't even in the running for fourth place, with Three Towers Preparatory beating them by two points.

As they sat down, a Wycliffe rider was leaving the ring on a striking black gelding. The noise the Wycliffe fan base made was nothing compared with the racket from the Saint Kits home crowd when their final rider trotted into the arena.

"Last to go, we have Caleb Meadows on Pageant's Pride, riding for Saint Christophers," came the announcement over the loudspeaker.

As Malory leaned forward to watch him canter the iron-gray gelding in a circle, she realized she was nervous for Caleb. Even if he was dating Patience, she still wanted him to ride well.

"If he goes clear, then Saint Kits will place second," Honey murmured as Caleb rode at the first fence.

"Hey, you guys, who does he remind you of?" Lani whispered as the gray horse flew over the jump and headed for the second fence.

Honey nodded. "I know! It's amazing."

"Who?" Malory whispered, not taking her eyes off the horse and rider below.

"You!" Lani told her.

"She's right." Dylan explained, "Look at the way he sits, and holds his hands, and hardly interferes with the horse once he's committed to the stride. That's exactly how you ride. I guess it makes sense since you both had the same instructor."

"Well, let's hope that doesn't mean he's going to go off course," Malory muttered, embarrassed by their praise and the comparison.

The gray horse did a huge, bold jump over the vertical; but as he was coming back down, he hit the top pole with his back legs and sent it thudding to the floor.

"Oh, no!" Lani said, as all of the Saint Kits fans groaned. "That means they're tied with Wycliffe again."

Malory continued to concentrate on Caleb's ride. After the stile, the horse and rider seemed to find their pace.

As Caleb cantered toward the combination, Malory held her breath. She so wanted Caleb to finish the last jump with no more faults. The gray pricked his ears and easily cleared the first fence. He then gave a perfect bounce stride that set him up to clear the second fence with a strong, rounded jump.

As Caleb patted the gray's neck, the Saint Kits crowd jumped to their feet. He had guaranteed Saint Kits a tie for second.

Wolf whistles and cheers echoed around the stadium. Malory was caught up in the energy and excitement.

Next time, she thought as she grabbed hold of a corner of Lani's Chestnut Hill flag to wave in the air and smiled at Dylan. *Next time, they'll be cheering for us!*

🐾

Malory looked around the walled courtyard where Saint Kits had set up an outdoor buffet for all the teams. Tables laden with food lined one wall, and staff were serving hot chocolate beside the ornate fountain in the center of the courtyard. Malory had left her friends to get a second cheesecake brownie and now couldn't find them anywhere. The courtyard was totally crowded with all of the competitors, supporters, and riding staff.

She glanced through a redbrick archway. It led to the courtyard that was at the center of the Saint Kits stables. Malory wondered if her friends had ventured in that direction.

"Malory!" Ms. Carmichael appeared by her side.

Malory forced herself to smile, even though her heart was sinking. She had tried to forget about her earlier ride, but now she'd have to face the facts. *This is when she tells me Tybalt's time is up.*

"I'll get right to the point so you can get back to the party," said Ms. Carmichael.

Malory nodded.

"I'm going to ask Mr. Ryan if he would be willing to extend Tybalt's loan period," Ms. Carmichael said briskly. "You've done well to bring Tybalt this far, and I feel you've earned a chance to finish what you've started. Based on that incredible jump he gave over the practice fence, I'm up for waiting to see what else he can do. And, as you know, we are looking for another pony for the team."

Malory stared at her instructor in disbelief.

"Malory?" Ms. Carmichael frowned. "Did you hear what I said? Do you want to keep training with Tybalt?"

Malory searched for her voice. "Yes, yes, oh, yes!" She had to stop herself from throwing her arms around the Director of Riding. Tybalt had gotten another chance! And so had she. This was one partnership she believed in, and she wanted to make it work.

"Okay then, we'll call Mr. Ryan tomorrow." Ms. Carmichael's eyes twinkled. "Enjoy the rest of the party."

Malory spun around to look for her friends to tell them the amazing news when someone touched her shoulder. Malory turned again, sloshing her cup of hot chocolate. "Sorry," she gasped, looking at the beads of liquid that were dribbling down a green team fleece in front of her.

She looked up into a pair of bright blue eyes, and suddenly her cheeks felt like they were on fire. "Caleb!" She tried to brush off the drops and instead turned them into dark smears.

"It's okay," he said, looking a little flustered himself. "I need to get it washed anyway."

Malory didn't know what to say, so she took a sip of the remaining hot chocolate.

"I just wanted to tell you that I thought you had a tough ride today," he rushed.

"Oh," Malory said, completely thrown.

"That didn't come out right," he said. "I meant that even though your pony was nervous, you handled him really well. You looked like you have a real bond with him."

Malory felt a rush of warmth. "Thanks," she smiled. "He's really special, but he's still working through some stuff." Suddenly she found herself telling Caleb about Tybalt's history, from the moment that she'd found him cowering in the barn to how she'd joined up with him. It wasn't just that she was making excuses for his behavior in the collecting ring; she knew Caleb would be genuinely interested in everything that had happened.

"You did a join-up with Amy Fleming?" His eyes opened wide, and Malory tried to tell herself they weren't the exact color of the sky on a summer's day.

"I know," she said. "I still can't believe it, either!"

"Wow." He shook his head. "I was so into that stuff she was saying at the symposium —" He broke off as Patience walked over and slipped her arm through his.

"Hey, you! I've been looking for you everywhere," she said, smiling coyly up at Caleb and ignoring Malory.

"Um, I'd better go check on Tybalt," Malory said, not wanting to hang around for fear she might get an uncontrollable urge to throw the rest of her hot chocolate on Patience's cashmere top.

"Mal!" Caleb called after her, but she didn't look back. She put her plate and cup down on the edge of the fountain and hurried through the double-gated entrance.

Malory slowed to a walk when she hit the paddock, going over her conversation with Caleb and making sure she hadn't said anything that suggested she thought of him as more than a friend. She knew he definitely qualified as that — a friend. It had been so easy to talk with him, and he was so interested in Tybalt. But remembering the way Patience had moved in on him like some kind of homing pigeon, she realized it was unlikely that she'd get to hang out with him anytime soon.

"Hey, Mal! We've all been looking for you." Dylan was walking away from the trailer. "Honey and Lani are probably searching under the buffet tables as I speak!"

Malory smiled. "I just thought I'd check on Tybalt. I want to tell him the best news!"

"What?" Dylan's eyes widened as she grabbed Malory's arm. "He's staying?"

"Almost definitely." Malory told her what Ms. Carmichael had said.

"That *is* the best news!" Dylan exclaimed. "Except for the fact that you'll probably want to sleep in the stable to spend more time bonding with him now." She laughed as Malory swatted at her.

"How dare you!" Malory exclaimed. "Don't give me ideas."

She walked up to Tybalt, who was tied in between Skylark and Shamrock.

"Hey, boy," she murmured. "I've brought you something." She held out the small piece of brownie she'd saved. "Just don't tell Ms. Carmichael I'm feeding you treats."

Tybalt gently lipped the cake off her hand and half closed his eyes as she rubbed his forehead. She knew she would do just about anything to help Tybalt be his best, but today, she was content to know he had a home at Chestnut Hill — at least for the foreseeable future. "You're staying," she murmured, leaning up close to him. "You're staying."

🐎

Dylan and Malory weaved through the trailers and cut across the drive back to the courtyard. "Do you want to look for Honey and Lani in the arena stands or the stable?" Dylan suggested.

"The stable," Malory said. She'd only got a peek at the brick barn, and it looked fabulous. She was sure Honey and Lani would have headed there to search for her — and even if they hadn't, she wanted a closer inspection.

The stable was picture-perfect. The roofs were neatly tiled in shades of red, and every box stall was wide, roomy, and equipped with self-watering buckets. Malory noticed the beautiful gray horse that Caleb had ridden, looking out over the nearest stable door. She wandered over to say hi.

The gray disappeared back into his stall to pull at his hay net before she reached him. Malory leaned over the door, admiring the well-bred gelding.

"Dutch Warmblood?" Dylan guessed, joining her.

"Looks like," Malory agreed, remembering his big bold jump. She frowned at the sound of raised voices coming from the tack room on the other side of the aisle.

"Is that Patience?" Dylan whispered.

Malory tilted her head, trying to hear better.

"All I'm saying is that you seemed to have a lot to talk about for just being friends!" As the voice became louder, it was clear it belonged to Patience.

"Look, Patience. We were just having a conversation. I would never tell you who you can and can't hang out with," a familiar voice replied. "But you might want to give it some thought yourself."

Malory's heart sped up as she realized Patience was talking to Caleb. She stared at Dylan, who put her finger to her lips, warning Malory to stay quiet.

"What's that supposed to mean?" Patience snapped.

"Well. It's just a rumor, but I heard Lynsey reported Dylan Walsh on her late-night ride. She had to have known Dylan would get caught," Caleb said.

Dylan grabbed Malory's arm. Malory guessed what she was wondering: How did Caleb hear that it was Lynsey? But neither spoke, anticipating Patience's response.

"Lynsey didn't set Dylan up," Patience said.

"Yeah, right," Caleb replied in a voice that made it clear he didn't believe her.

"Well, she didn't," Patience threw back at him. "It was me. I told our housemother."

There was a stunned silence. Malory and Dylan looked at each other. Dylan's mouth fell open, her hazel eyes darkening. It had been Patience all along?

"Why did you do that?" Caleb asked, taking his time with each word.

"Because Dylan was after Lynsey from the start," Patience said. "She deserved some of what she was dishing out. Lynsey never did anything to her."

"So you decided to even things out?" Caleb sounded totally frozen. "You've got a sick sense of loyalty, Patience." There was the sound of footsteps walking out of the tack room. Malory and Dylan shrank back against the wall.

"Where are you going?" Patience called.

"I'm going back to the party. I want to hang out with some of my friends," Caleb said heavily.

Malory's feet were rooted to the ground. The last thing she wanted was for Caleb to know she'd overheard the conversation, but she didn't want him to see her high-tailing it across the yard, either. And Dylan clearly wasn't going anywhere. She looked ready to give Patience an exceptionally evil eye.

Caleb stepped out of the tack room, his face flushed. He stared at Malory in dismay when he saw her practically hugging the stable wall.

"Hi, Caleb. We were just checking out your horse," she rushed. *Oh, great. How many more awkward moments can I have with this guy?*

Caleb gave a small smile. "His name's Pageant's Pride, but we call him Gent around the barn."

"What, as in, 'he's a real classy gent'?" Dylan asked, but she wasn't looking at Caleb. She was staring at the tack room door.

Caleb gave Dylan a funny look. "Well, I guess so."

He broke off as Patience appeared. Her eyes were downcast, and Malory felt a stab of sympathy for her. She could hardly blame Patience for liking Caleb, but she couldn't believe she was the one who had told Mrs. Herson about Dylan's dare.

Patience looked from Caleb to Malory to Dylan, her face draining of color. "Did you hear all that?" she whispered.

"Every single word," Dylan said, crossing her arms.

Patience bit her lower lip and, without saying anything else, hurried across the yard.

"I'd better find out if she's okay," Caleb said, sounding uncomfortable.

Malory nodded and turned back to look at Pageant's Pride. In a way, she was glad Caleb went after Patience; it proved he was the kind of guy she had always thought he was. She didn't fully understand why Patience had decided to tell on Dylan — especially not if it was to stand up for Lynsey — but she was sure Patience needed someone to talk to now that the news was out.

"There's Honey and Lani!" Dylan said in a conspiratory tone. "How's that for perfect timing? They'll never believe what we just heard. Find us when you're done!"

Malory turned around in time to see Dylan racing out of the stables to meet their friends, who had just appeared in the courtyard. Then, to her surprise, she saw Caleb was still standing next to her.

"Hey." He looked down and scuffed at the cobbles with his boot. "I was wondering if we could maybe meet up sometime soon, maybe for coffee after Thanksgiving? I'd really like to hear more about what you did with Tybalt."

Malory felt a rush of excitement. "I'm not sure," she said, trying to keep her voice steady.

Caleb shrugged. "If you're worried about Patience,

please don't. We didn't exactly hit it off when we went out. We just didn't have anything to talk about."

Malory smiled. She knew that finding something to talk about wouldn't be a problem for them. "Um, okay then."

"So is that a yes?" Caleb grinned.

"That's a yes," Malory agreed, her heart pounding.

"I'll find you later so we can swap numbers and all that," Caleb said.

Malory nodded. She could have sworn she saw him blush before he turned away.

"Later," Malory called.

She watched him stride off and then crossed the court-yard to meet her friends, who were pretending to study the horses in the stalls with great intensity.

"So?" Dylan asked.

"He just asked me if I wanted to have coffee," Malory answered demurely.

"That's a date!" Dylan and Lani yelled at the same time.

Malory felt uncertain. Caleb had just said coffee, but Honey seemed to be giving her a knowing look, too.

"'Coffee' is the international code word for a casual date," Honey confirmed.

"He's totally cute. Does he have any friends?" Lani asked.

"Yeah, maybe he has three," Dylan joked. "We'll take up an entire row at the movie theater!"

"He only asked me to coffee!" Malory declared, but

she laughed along with her friends. "I'll see what I can do after Thanksgiving."

Honey's face suddenly became serious. "Hang on, you guys. What are we going to do over Thanksgiving?" she asked abruptly. "It's going to be so weird not seeing you for a whole week."

Vacation was starting in just three days. Malory could guess what they were all thinking because she felt exactly the same way. As much as she wanted to go home and be with her dad, part of her wanted to stay at Chestnut Hill, too.

Dylan gave an exaggerated sigh. "I guess I'm going to just have to console myself with second helpings of all my mom's home-cooked meals."

Malory thought back to Thanksgiving last year; the first without her mom. She'd never thought then that so much happiness lay just around the corner. Her friends had been so supportive over the last months, and she was starting to develop a stronger sense of trust — just as Tybalt was. And she had a feeling things would only get better! With some more time, Tybalt might find himself truly at home at Chestnut Hill, and thriving with the competition of the junior jumping team. Malory would do everything she could to help him, but she was also prepared to let him go if he would be happier somewhere else.

"I have an idea," Honey said as they made their way

through the courtyard and toward the Chestnut Hill trailer. "How about we all agree to think of one another when we're having our Thanksgiving dinner?"

"Yeah, let's do it. We can all know we're thinking about one another — about us," Lani agreed.

"To us!" they chorused, pretending to clink invisible glasses in the air.

Malory caught Dylan's eye and grinned. *So much for the Three Musketeers — four is a much better number!*

They wandered over to the Chestnut Hill trailer, where the ponies were dozing.

At the sound of their voices, Tybalt swung his head around. He let out a low whinny when he recognized Malory. She smiled and went over to put her face against his neck.

"Just you wait until after Thanksgiving," she whispered, still feeling as excited about Ali's decision as when she had first heard it. "We're going to have a lot of fun together." And now, the pictures in her head weren't of racing Tybalt against the clock in jumping competitions, but of working steadily in the ring, building on the bond that Amy Fleming had started with the join-up session, and making her partnership with Tybalt as real and solid as it could possibly be.

Tybalt closed his eyes while Malory scratched his forehead.

"So," Dylan said, breaking into her thoughts. "Isn't there somewhere you should be?"

"I don't know what you mean," Malory replied.

"Come on," Lani said, grabbing Malory's hand. "If I'm not mistaken, Ms. O'Neil has some numbers to swap with a certain boy from Saint Kits. And, once we're done with that, we need to show Allbrights that the Chestnut Hill girls know how to party, even when we don't come in first."

As they walked back across the field, Malory glanced at her three friends and felt herself smiling from ear to ear.

The Chestnut Hill girls. She liked the sound of that. It was the sound of belonging.

Hiding a Secret Close to Her Heart

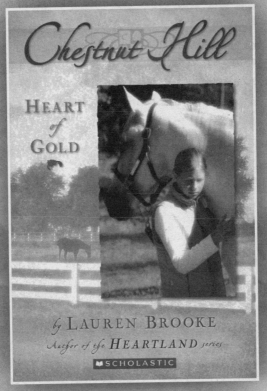

When a pony is injured at Chestnut Hill, Honey devotes herself to nursing it back to health. But the pony belongs to Patience, who has done little to earn the trust of the other girls. Honey's friends don't know why helping the pony is so important to Honey. If only they knew her secret, they would begin to understand.

www.scholastic.com/chestnuthill

CH3